"I'm impressed by how you handled that teenager."

"Wow, can I get a junior FBI badge or something?"

"Don't push it."

Garrett looked surprised, as if he hadn't meant to utter the playful retort. Lana thought he might have even cracked a smile but couldn't be sure. It would be a vast improvement on his permanent frown, his lips stretched into a thin straight line.

"I'd like to ask a favor of you," he said.

"Sure."

"Promise me you'll never do that again?"

"You mean..."

"Insinuate yourself into a dangerous situation like that."

Lana dunked her tea bag in the hot water and sighed. He was asking the impossible. She couldn't turn her back on someone who was in so much pain they were blinded to the beauty of life and the grace of God. She knew how precious life was, and how short it could be.

"I'm sorry, I can't make that promise," she said.

Books by Hope White

Love Inspired Suspense

Hidden in Shadows
Witness on the Run
Christmas Haven
Small Town Protector

HOPE WHITE

An eternal optimist, Hope was born and raised in the Midwest. She began spinning tales of intrigue and adventure when she was in grade school, and wrote her first book when she was eleven—a thriller that ended with a mysterious phone call the reader never heard!

She and her college sweetheart have been married for thirty years and are blessed with two wonderful sons, two feisty cats and a bossy border collie.

When not dreaming up inspirational tales, Hope enjoys hiking, sipping tea with friends and going to the movies. She loves to hear from readers, who can contact her at hopewhiteauthor@gmail.com.

Small Town
Protector

HOPE WHITE

Love Inspired

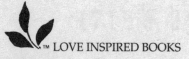 LOVE INSPIRED BOOKS

Recycling programs
for this product may
not exist in your area.

ISBN-13: 978-0-373-67519-7

SMALL TOWN PROTECTOR

Copyright © 2012 by Pat White

www.LoveInspiredBooks.com

Printed in U.S.A.

For my dad, Lou,
who is practically perfect in every way.

Faith is the substance of things hoped for,
the evidence of things not seen.
—*Hebrews* 11:1

ONE

The night cruises Lana offered to Salish Island were usually her favorite. But something felt off tonight.

Maybe it was the confrontation with a tourist who tried to bribe his way onto her boat, even after she'd explained they'd reached their capacity. Or maybe it was the sudden breeze that sent goose bumps down her arms. A sign of an unexpected storm and they should head back?

Yet right now it was so peaceful out here. She and her teenage staff had set up the tiki lights, food and hot beverages. Her guests were having a great time toasting hot dogs and marshmallows over the crackling campfire. A little girl climbed onto her daddy's lap and he handed her a stick to wave over the fire.

Lana hated to cut the visit short, but safety was her number one priority. She'd call Anderson Greene for an update. The sailing fanatic was obsessed with the weather.

"Hello," he answered, a bit out of breath.

"Hey, Anderson, it's Lana. You okay?"

"Yep, just harder to get around with the sciatica acting up."

"I'm sorry."

"What can I do for you?"

"What's the scoop on the weather tonight?"

"You're not scheduling a trip to Salish, are you?"

"We're already on island, why?"

"There's a front coming in from the north. Last I heard…fifty-mile-an-hour—"

The line went dead.

"Anderson?"

Loss of communication, not a good sign. She decided to play it safe and head back. She'd give her customers coupons for her snack shop, Stone Soup, to make up for having to leave the island early.

Glancing across the group, she caught sight of her teenage helpers, Ashley and Sketch. They held hands as Sketch dangled a marshmallow over the flame.

Melancholy washed over Lana, but only for a second. She'd made herself a promise not to let the darkness consume her like it had years ago after Dad died.

Taking a deep breath, she forced a smile and wandered to the group of tourists.

"Hey, guys. This will have to be your last marshmallow. The weather's a little quirky so we're going to head back."

A middle-aged couple stood, ready to go; a mom and dad with three kids encouraged them to finish their toasting; Ashley and Sketch shared a quick kiss and then started packing up supplies.

Lana did a quick head count. Odd. They were two short. She counted again. Sixteen, including herself. The boat's capacity was seventeen plus Lana, which meant two people had wandered off. She checked her list of tourists on her smartphone. Yep, just as she thought: the teenage couple must have wandered off. Although she'd asked the guests to stay within sight of the campfire, she knew that some teens suffered from selective hearing.

She motioned to Sketch and Ashley. "We're two short. Sketch, come with me."

She grabbed a lantern and motioned him toward the trail leading to the north side of the island. Sketch glanced over his shoulder. The full moon illuminated the playful smile he shot back at Ashley.

"You guys are adorable," Lana said. And truth be told, she was a bit envious.

She missed being in a relationship, having someone join her for a movie or hiking adventure in the nearby state park. Yet being in the wrong relationship was worse than being alone. She'd learned that the hard way during her eight months with Vincent.

"Why are we going this way?" Sketch asked.

"I'm guessing they went to Lover's Point."

"Why?"

"I was a teenager once." A regretful smile played across her lips at the memory of young love. She often wished she hadn't pushed Gregory away back in high school. But then, she'd fallen into a dark place after Dad had died and had pretty much pushed everyone away.

"If you and Ashley were out here alone, basking in the glow of a full moon, wouldn't you head for the most romantic spot in the Pacific Northwest?" she teased.

A shrill scream cut through the air. Lana froze for a second. Did she really hear…?

A second scream echoed from the north end of the island. Lana and Sketch instinctively rushed toward the source of the sound. They zipped around Quinault Rock and spotted the two teenagers standing at the shoreline. The boy held his girlfriend in his arms, patting her back. Maybe they'd just had a fight?

"You guys okay?" Lana asked, out of breath.

Sketch poked Lana's shoulder, then pointed at the water.

Lana glanced down…

Into the face of a bloated dead body.

What a fool. The man actually thought he could swim five miles back to Port Whisper from the island? In his shape?

It had been a mistake to hunt so close to home. I realize that now. But I couldn't help myself. I saw how Rick Washburn bullied his female, how they fought, how he made her cry….

Adrenaline had surged through my body. It had been a month since I deleted Lars Gunderson. Too long. So I lured Ricky to the island for a private tour.

Unfortunately he didn't enjoy my game of control and defeat.

He ran. Dove. Drowned.

And now the Feds will invade my charming little town.
A pleasant, boring town. Just the way I like it.

But not anymore, not with the FBI sniffing around,
trying to find me.

I'll have to take care of that; redirect their attention.
Not so close to home this time.

FBI agent Garrett Drake couldn't believe his current case had led him back to Port Whisper where the memories still burned fresh in his mind, and even more painful in his chest.

He'd think God was playing a trick on him except he didn't believe in God. Not after everything he'd seen. Not after everything he'd lost.

Shove it back, way back.

His escort, Scooner Locke, pulled the motorboat up to the dock, and a man tied them off. Garrett didn't like involving civilians, but the chief and his staff were all at the scene. Garrett jumped out of the boat and started up the dock. If the body was really Rick Washburn's…

It was a game changer.

The killer had altered his pattern, which meant either he'd made a mistake—which would put Garrett that much closer to nailing him—or the killer was escalating.

Which made him less predictable and twice as dangerous.

"Special Agent Drake?" A man approached him. "I'm Chief Morgan Wright."

They shook hands. The chief, mid-thirties, wore black jeans, a denim jacket and a Mariners baseball cap. He was probably off duty when he got the call.

"It's up that hill on the left." The chief led him along a trail.

"Who found him?"

"Two teenagers."

"What were they doing out here at night?" Garrett asked.

"They were part of a tour group."

"People tour the island at night?"

"Yep, they roast hot dogs and marshmallows around a campfire, tell ghost stories, that sort of thing. Lana started it about a year ago. It's very popular."

"Lana?"

"My sister-in-law, Lana Burns. She runs boat tours to the island out of her snack shop, Stone Soup. She's the one who called in the body."

The body. Possibly the latest victim of the Red Hollow Killer, a name inspired by the type of rope he used to strangle his vics.

The minute Garrett got the call that a floater looked a lot like his missing person, he'd busted tail to get to the scene. He didn't want it to be Washburn, and not just because it meant Red Hollow went off script. It would also mean the killer had been here and maybe still was.

In the same town as Caroline, Garrett's former mother-in-law.

Garrett's ex-wife and son had lost enough thanks

to his job. He wouldn't allow them to lose a loving mother and grandmother, as well.

"If it's Rick Washburn, the killer's victimology has changed," Garrett explained. "Which means he's escalating, making him unpredictable and potentially more dangerous."

"Changed, how?"

"Up to now, the victims are kidnapped and a ransom note is sent to the family, giving them, and us, the illusion that the victim can be saved. But before the ransom drop takes place, he leads us to the body, which is posed with very specific items. An empty bourbon bottle, cigar and black leather belt. The victim has been strangled with red hollow braided rope. Lab results indicate he's been drugged with an oxy cocktail. I'm assuming, since Washburn floated up on shore, you didn't find a bourbon bottle, cigar or belt near or on the victim?"

"No, sir."

"Were there signs he'd been strangled?"

"Not that I could tell."

"We know he was the next victim, yet he wasn't posed or strangled. Do you have any idea why Washburn was in Port Whisper?"

"He checked into the Blue Goose Motel alone, but was seen around town with a female, brunette, mid-forties."

"Probably a mistress. He has a history of cheating on his wife. Why didn't she report him missing? We got the ransom email two days ago."

"A witness saw them fighting, and later that night another witness saw her convertible peel out of the parking lot. They came in separate cars."

"You've gathered a lot of information in the last hour."

"Small-town grapevine. Sometimes it comes in handy."

As they approached the scene, Garrett noticed a young woman sitting on a rock, a wool blanket draped across her shoulders. Long, light brown hair floated down her back. Garrett thought she was trembling, but couldn't be sure.

"Is that one of the teenagers who found the victim?" Garrett asked.

"No, it's Lana. You want to talk to her?"

"I'd like to see the body first."

Garrett strode to the body and the chief introduced him to his deputy.

"Deputy Finnegan, this is Special Agent Drake from the FBI's Behavioral Analysis Unit."

They shook hands.

"Good to meet you," Finnegan said.

"Likewise." Garrett snapped on a pair of gloves and crouched beside the body. Resignation washed over him. "It's Washburn." Fully clothed in a dress shirt, khaki pants and windbreaker. "Did you find red braided rope anywhere in the vicinity of where you pulled him from the water?"

"No, sir."

Garrett turned Washburn's head slightly. No ligature marks. Washburn was the next victim, yet at first glance this looked like an accidental drowning.

"I'm assuming your forensics team processed the scene before you pulled him out?" Garrett asked.

"Not yet."

Garrett glanced at Chief Wright for an explanation.

"We're a small town," he said. "A county forensics team is on the way."

Garrett didn't want inexperience to mess up this investigation, but he knew things would go more smoothly if he worked with local law enforcement instead of being at odds with them.

"I'd like to speak with the forensics team as soon as they arrive." Garrett stood and snapped off his gloves. "Where are the teenagers who found the body?"

"They went back to town with the tour group," a light voice said.

Garrett turned to its source: Lana Burns. She rolled her neck and looked up at him with round, tired eyes.

"Who authorized that?" he asked the chief.

"I sent them back," Lana answered, standing. "The kids were completely freaked, so I figured the sooner they went home, the sooner they'd calm down. They'll be more helpful if they're calm, right?"

She stepped up to him, a little too close for his taste, and he noticed her eyes were a remarkable shade of golden-green; her skin was flawless.

"What's your email address?" she asked, focusing on her smartphone.

He didn't answer at first, trying to figure out how

someone who saw a dead body—he assumed her first—could be so calm, so…lovely.

Man, he needed about a week of sleep.

She glanced up, expectant. "I'll email you the contact information for everyone on the tour tonight."

He handed her a business card, then pulled a small notebook from the breast pocket of his suit.

"How about you?" he said.

She reached for his notebook and he found himself handing it to her. "Here are all my numbers. Cell, landline and the snack shop."

"Are you too *freaked* to answer some questions?"

She handed him back the notebook. "Nope. Go for it."

"Is this a usual thing, bringing people out here late at night?"

"It was only seven." She planted her hands on her hips in self-defense. "I would never bring people out here if I didn't think it was safe."

"I wasn't inferring—"

"I mean, I've been hosting the night cruises for a year now and we've never had any problems. People love sitting around a campfire and singing songs, roasting marshmallows and telling stories. I guess it reminds them of childhood or something. Happier times. Well, that and it's breathtaking out here, quiet and peaceful, usually peaceful, but not so peaceful when a couple of teenagers find a dead body and—" She stopped midsentence. "Sorry."

"For what?"

"Rambling. I do that when I'm nervous."

"Am I making you nervous?"

"Of course you are."

Garrett glanced up from his notepad, puzzled, and waited for her to continue her rambling. He found it... endearing. *Focus, Drake.*

"You're tall and intimidating and your tone is, well, accusatory," she said.

"Sorry." Now she had him apologizing. "Back to my questions, do you usually bring your group to this part of the island?"

"Why shouldn't I?"

"Miss Burns, I'm not accusing you of any impropriety." However, he sensed that, no matter how politely he phrased his questions, he'd already put her on the defensive. He'd try a different tact. He refocused on his notebook. "Do people sign up for the tour in advance?"

"Usually, yes, although tonight I had some guy try to muscle in at the last minute."

"Can you give me a description?"

"About sixty, five-nine or -ten, on the rotund side, with thinning brown hair and thick sunglasses. I never trust a person who won't look me in the eye."

Garrett instinctively looked up. "You have good instincts."

"Wow, thanks."

He ripped his gaze from her striking eyes and jotted down the description. "What was his demeanor?"

"Bossy, rude, maybe a little desperate."

"Desperate?" Garrett's hand froze on the page.

"Yeah, he had that look like if he didn't get over here his world was going to end."

Could it have been Red Hollow? Did he fear he hadn't securely anchored his victim and knew he'd float to the surface prematurely? If this was the case, Lana Burns had seen him, up close.

"What's wrong?" she asked.

He glanced up and found her studying him with wide, golden-green eyes like she was reading his thoughts.

"What's the schedule once you dock?" he asked, changing the subject.

"On day trips we spread out blankets and have a picnic, and for the night tours we roast wieners and marshmallows to make s'mores. I tell stories about the island and its history, the Nahali myth about an Indian girl who was saved from a freak storm by a fisherman and how they fell in love even though there was no way they could be together. Sometimes I'll take the group up to Lover's Point, usually not at night. The teenagers who found the body couldn't resist, I guess."

Of course not, they were young, romantic and naive.

As she rambled on, he put her in the naive category by the tone of her voice: hopeful and innocent. She had no idea of the danger she could have encountered tonight. He wasn't sure how to tell her, or if he even should.

No, knowledge was ammunition.

"Miss Burns—"

"Lana."

"Lana, I don't want to alarm you, but I'm here because we've been tracking a serial killer."

"I know, Morgan told me."

Garrett glanced at Chief Wright and back to Lana.

"He's my brother-in-law," Lana explained.

"That's great, but I'd rather the whole town not know about our case."

"Uh, it's probably too late. Small towns." She shrugged.

Garrett took a deep breath. "At any rate, we have to consider the man you turned away tonight as a suspect."

"You mean the serial killer?"

"Yes."

"I doubt it."

"Why's that?"

"Aren't serial killers supposed to be smart? He didn't seem very smart, or very organized…."

Garrett sensed anxiety inspired her new round of rambling. She'd possibly been inches from a murderer. That realization would make anyone nervous.

Making direct eye contact, he touched her shoulder. "It's okay. I'm not going to let anything happen to you."

"Really," she said, cynicism lacing her voice.

Not the response he expected. He removed his hand. "I'm sorry, I've offended you again?"

"No, it's fine. I've had people make promises lately and, well, never mind. What else do you need from me?" She eyed his notebook.

"Tell me about tonight, when you found the body, if it's not too upsetting."

"We were going to head back because of a change in the weather, but were missing two teenagers, so Sketch and I went looking for them."

"Sketch?"

"The teenager who helps me out. I figured the kids headed up to Lover's Point, so we came up here and heard a scream and found the couple and the dead body. That's pretty much it."

"You don't seem that upset by the sight of a dead body."

"It's not my first."

"Excuse me?"

"My dad. I was twelve."

"Oh, sorry."

Man, he kept stepping into trouble with this woman.

"But it's weird, ya know, I mean, first the hole, then a dead body," Lana said.

"What hole?"

"Up by Quinault Rock. Some animal or person digs a five-foot hole in the middle of an uninhabited island. What's that about?"

Garrett glanced in the direction of the rock. "Interesting."

"Not so interesting when you're stuck down there for hours."

He snapped his attention to her.

"Yes, I fell into a hole. Literally. No jokes, please."

"I don't joke."

"Doesn't surprise me." She slapped her hand to her mouth. "I can't believe I just said that. Sorry, I've been up since five and haven't eaten anything substantial since, I don't know, noon?"

"Why don't you go on back to town? I'll find you if I have more questions."

"Great. Here's my card." She dug a colorful card out of her jeans pocket and passed it to him.

"Hey, Morgan," she called. "Can I catch a ride back?"

Garrett motioned to the chief. "I'd like you to have one of your deputies escort Miss Burns back to town. I'm concerned about her safety."

"Why?"

"She may have seen the killer."

"Lana, you didn't tell me—"

"It was some guy I turned away earlier tonight. It's probably nothing."

"Scott," Chief Wright motioned his deputy over.

"No, Morgan, don't," Lana said. "I'll be safe with Scooner."

"I'd rather not involve civilians," Garrett said.

"He's a former SEAL and Town Safety captain. She'll be safe with him."

Garrett acquiesced. "Please ask him to escort her all the way home," Garrett suggested.

"Will do," the chief said. "Forensics just docked."

Garrett nodded at Lana. "Thank you, Miss Burns."

Lana pulled the blanket tighter around her shoulders. "Good night, Agent Drake."

With an arm around her shoulder, Chief Wright

walked her past the forensics team, who made their way up the hill to the crime scene. Garrett fought the urge to call out one last warning, to ask if she had pepper spray or suggest she stay with a family member tonight.

Not good. He had to stop letting his protective instincts distract him and focus on finding Red Hollow. He could still be here, in Port Whisper, a threat to innocents like Lana.

A threat to his son's grandmother.

The pain of losing his family rushed to the surface. Being back in Port Whisper where he'd asked for Olivia's hand in marriage, where they'd planned a future they'd never have, was messing with him. Big-time.

It was distracting his focus from tracking a killer and protecting a fragile innocent, Lana Burns. The best thing he could do for her and everyone in town was leave the past behind and focus on the case.

Yet he needed to stop by his former mother-in-law's place. He owed Caroline more respect than to have her find out about his presence in town through the gossip mill.

The experience wouldn't be a pleasant one. He was sure she hadn't forgiven him, and he couldn't blame her. His ambition, his workaholic nature inherited from his father, put his wife and, at the time, three-year-old son in danger fourteen years ago.

"Agent Drake?"

Garrett snapped his attention to Deputy Finnegan.

"This is our forensic investigator, Oliver Marsh," he introduced. They shook hands.

With a slow, deep breath, Garrett shoved his personal connections to this town away, locking the door. Analyzing his mistakes and regrets would only distract him from his most critical goal: finding the elusive killer before he struck again.

An hour later the forensic investigator offered his preliminary opinion: time of death was between 3:00 and 7:00 p.m.; there was dirt and blood under Washburn's fingernails as if he had tried to claw his way out of something; and he'd most likely drowned. He wasn't strangled like the rest of the victims.

That change in pattern disturbed Garrett the most. His team relied on the profile, designed to help them determine what the killer might do next, to whom and where.

They docked at Port Whisper and the forensic techs took the body to the lab where they'd continue their analysis. The chief took Garrett to meet with the teenagers who found the body, but they couldn't offer anything helpful. They were still traumatized by the image of the dead man's eyes staring up at them.

It was quarter past eleven. Garrett was tired, hungry and frustrated.

"I don't suppose anything's open this time of night?" he asked as the chief drove Garrett back to his car.

"Actually, the Turnstyle is open until midnight. Up Main Street about four blocks."

"Thanks."

The chief pulled over. "I'm assuming you'll come by the office in the morning?"

"Yes."

"Do you have a place to sleep tonight?"

"I'll find something."

"You could always try Caroline Ross's place, the Port Whisper Inn. It's quiet and homey."

And loaded with land mines.

"Thanks."

"See you tomorrow." The chief shook Garrett's hand.

Garrett sensed the man was honorable and had decent instincts for a small-town cop. "Good night."

Walking through town to the restaurant, Garrett called team member Georgia Hunt and told her to send a forensic artist to Port Whisper, but there was no reason the entire team should join him just yet. They should stay in Tacoma and continue to work leads from the previous murder.

Garrett, on the other hand, wasn't going anywhere until he felt confident his former mother-in-law wasn't in danger.

He could swing by the inn now, but it was late and he didn't want to alarm her. Like a morning visit would be any less alarming? She probably never expected to see or hear from him again, maybe even hoped…

But he knew in his heart that sending Olivia and Steven into protective custody had been the only way to protect them from the serial killer that had made Garrett a target.

A year later, Olivia had filed for divorce. Truth was, their marriage started to crumble about the same time his career took off, shortly after Steven was born. Garrett threw himself into work to provide for his family, and Olivia accused him of being a workaholic, absent, aloof.

Like his old man.

Garrett hadn't planned to become a workaholic like his father, but the job quickly consumed him. They'd solve a case, and another would pop onto the radar. They'd save a victim, but lose three more.

His work ethic intensified once the divorce was final and Garrett had no one to think about but himself.

That wasn't true. He thought about Steven. Every single day of his life.

Three years after he'd put his wife and son into the program, the killer who'd targeted Garrett was shot eluding police. The threat gone, Garrett could safely see his son, who'd just turned six. Yet Olivia said if Garrett truly loved Steven, he'd let her new husband raise him as his own. Garrett couldn't walk away that easily.

Heart pounding, he'd swung by Steven's baseball game and stood by the fence, watching as his son scored the winning run. The little guy was swarmed by teammates and when he broke free he rushed to his stepdad, Kurt, and slapped him a high five.

At that moment Garrett knew it was selfish to in-sinuate himself back into Steven's life. Steven had a new dad, one who'd always be there.

Garrett's son was better off without him, without a workaholic father unable to give him the time, guid-ance and love he so desperately needed. Garrett re-treated, as Olivia had requested.

It was the right thing to do. His former mother-in-law had to respect him for putting Steven's needs first, right?

"This town," he muttered, shutting off the flow of memories, questionable decisions and regrets. He couldn't let his emotions distract him from finding a serial killer.

The glow of florescent lights spilled onto the street from the Turnstyle Restaurant up ahead—a lot of ac-tivity for a small town this late at night. Then again, if they'd heard about the murder, they probably needed to get together and process. More like gossip. Garrett knew how small towns worked.

He pushed open the door to the restaurant and hes-itated, fearing someone would figure out he was the federal agent and ask him questions. A few people glanced up.

A female server with a name tag that read Anna approached him. "Table for one?"

"Yes, ma'am."

"Ma'am? So formal." She smiled and he tried to offer one in return but couldn't. She was not quite thirty with long, auburn hair tied back.

"Do you have a booth in the back?" he asked.

"Sure."

He followed her to the rear of the restaurant, slid into a booth, and she handed him a menu.

"Are you serving breakfast this time of night?" he asked.

"You bet. Boomer's blueberry pancakes are amazing."

"I'll keep that in mind."

"Start you off with something to drink?"

"Coffee would be great."

"Regular or decaf?"

"Regular, please."

She breezed off and he glanced at the menu, trying to look like a tourist in town for some R & R, something he'd rarely experienced in his adult life. Dressed in his crisp navy suit, starched white shirt and maroon tie, he looked nothing like a man on vacation.

From this vantage point he could see everything: a man in workman's clothes seated at the counter; Scooner Locke and two middle-aged men deep in conversation; a table of four raucous teenagers; and a young couple in the booth next to Garrett, blindly eating while an infant slept in a baby carrier next to them.

Anna returned with his coffee. "What can I get you?"

"I'll try the blueberry pancakes." He passed her the menu and closed his eyes, trying to relax the muscles coiling in his neck.

"Lana? Weren't you supposed to stay home tonight?"

Garrett opened his eyes and caught sight of the ethereal Lana Burns standing just inside the door.

One of the men at Scooner's table waved her over. "Come over here and give us the scoop on the…" He glanced around the restaurant and thought better of announcing to the room that a dead body had been discovered. "Come join us."

"No, you get back home," Scooner said. "I had orders to make sure you stayed there."

"Both of you stop bossing me around. I need to eat." She turned to Anna, who poured coffee for a customer at the counter. "How fast can Lew make me some pancakes?" Lana asked.

She wasn't supposed to be alone, wandering the streets late at night. She wasn't supposed to be so… enchanting. He had the urge to jump out of the booth and scold her for not following his order to stay home, but she'd been through enough tonight. She didn't need a lecture from Garrett. He'd wait until she'd finished her pancakes, then he'd follow her home to make sure she was safe.

Leaning across the counter, chatting with her friend, no one would ever guess Lana Burns had seen a dead body only hours ago. She cracked a full-blown smile that lit up her face. It took Garrett's breath away.

He pulled out his notebook and fought the distraction of her gentle voice drifting across the restaurant. Maybe it was time to consider dating again, pursuing a relationship that involved more than investigative theories and hunting killers.

Who was he kidding? There was no place in his life for romance. He'd never put someone he cared about in danger again, and as long as he worked for the FBI, that's exactly where they'd be.

Focusing on his notes, he hoped Lana didn't decide to join him for a late-night snack. He didn't have the energy to keep his protective shields up, and for some reason he needed them with this woman. What was it about her that rattled his focus?

She had no pretense. She said what she thought without reservation or censor. There was no guess-work with the petite beauty, no maneuvering to get what he needed. All he had to do was ask, and she'd answer him truthfully and more than a bit directly.

The restaurant door flew open and a teenage boy wearing a torn denim jacket and black baseball cap stormed inside. His bloodshot eyes frantically scanned the restaurant. Garrett's instincts spiked.

"Table for one?" Anna asked from behind the counter.

Lana turned to him and…

The kid whipped out a knife. "I need money."

TWO

Garrett automatically slid his hand inside his jacket to reach for his gun. The room went suddenly quiet except for the sound of the baby fussing in the booth next to him. He couldn't open fire, not with all these civilians in the room. The perp could easily use one as a shield.

"Money, yeah, don't we all," Lana joked. "I was about to have a plate of Boomer's blueberry pancakes, but it's always too much food. Wanna split it with me?"

The kid looked confused. "What?"

"Pancakes, you know, flour, milk, butter, lots of butter. Come on. Anna, put in an order of Boomer's for me, 'kay?" Lana wandered to the front booth, away from other customers.

Smart girl. One of the men in the booth up front shifted—the navy SEAL. Not good. If he jumped to the rescue, he could spook the kid. The thought of the teenager pressing the blade to Lana's throat made Garrett grip the Formica table. He had to get up there and diffuse the situation.

Lana sat down and smiled up at the teenager, actually smiled at a kid who was waving a knife in her face.

"Aren't you hungry? I'm starving," she said. "Haven't eaten since scones at lunch. Mom makes the best cranberry nut scones. Spread a little clotted cream on them and you're a fan for life. You've gotta try them sometime."

As she rattled on, Scooner started to shift out of the booth. Lana glanced at him and shook her head, encouraging him not to come to her rescue. Scooner hesitated on the edge of his seat.

"Anna, how about some tea?" she called across the restaurant, then redirected her attention to the kid. "Or do you prefer soda? They make the best cream sodas, my personal kryptonite. I could drink them for breakfast, lunch and dinner. And gain ten pounds in a week. Not good for someone who's barely five-three." She tapped on the table with her fingertips. "Come on, sit down."

The kid took a step toward the table, clutching the knife. Garrett's hand tingled with the need to draw his firearm.

"Don't you like pancakes?" she asked with innocent eyes.

"I don't have any money," the kid croaked.

"No problem. I've got a little extra tonight. We had a really good week on my tour boat. I take people over to Salish Island. Do you live around here? I'm a lifer but I don't remember meeting you. Sorry, I was probably your babysitter or something, right?" she joked.

"I'm not from here." The kid closed the knife and shoved it in his pocket.

Scooner stood.

"Sit down," Lana said.

The kid joined her in the booth, figuring she was talking to him.

"You, too, Scooner," she ordered, not breaking eye contact with the teenager.

"Where are you from?" she asked.

He shrugged.

"Well, besides having the best blueberry pancakes in the state of Washington, our state park has awesome trails if you like hiking, and sailing on Puget Sound is a blast. You ever been sailing?"

Was it just Garrett, or was she being incredibly trusting? Either that or he should hire her for his team.

The kid seemed to have calmed down, but Garrett couldn't be sure he'd stay that way. As Garrett swung his leg out of the booth, the front door opened. Deputy Finnegan stepped into the restaurant and approached Lana's table.

"Everything okay here?" he asked.

"Great. We're about to have pancakes, right?" She eyed the teen.

"Yeah." His shoulders slumped. He took out the knife and placed it on the table.

Deputy Finnegan motioned Lana out of the booth.

She took a few steps toward the counter, but she wasn't far enough away for Garrett's taste.

"Anything else in your pockets?" Finnegan asked the kid.

The teen pulled his pockets inside out. They were empty. Finnegan pocketed the knife.

"You'd better come with me."

The kid stood, head hung low, and Finnegan cuffed him.

"Wait, I didn't get your name," Lana said.

The kid glanced at her through long bangs. "Michael."

"Nice to meet you, Michael. I'll bring pancakes by the police station." She turned her attention to the deputy. "Is that okay, Scott?"

Garrett leaned back in his booth, his jaw dropping in disbelief.

"Sure," Deputy Finnegan said, shaking his head.

"Cool. I'll see you later, okay, Michael?"

Michael glanced over his shoulder, and that's when Garrett saw the tears streaming down the kid's face.

"You have something you want to say to Lana?" Finnegan asked.

"Thanks," he choked.

"Something else?" the cop prompted.

"Sorry."

"I forgive you," Lana said.

The deputy led Michael out of the restaurant.

Dead silence filled the restaurant. Lana glanced at the customers. "What?"

"What were you thinking?" Scooner challenged.

"I was thinking you were going to freak the kid out with your macho karate moves, and kick me in the head by mistake." One of the other guys at the table chuckled.

"Lana, I can't believe you did that." Anna darted around the counter and gave her a hug.

The young couple packed up their baby and left cash on the table, the teenagers burst into a frenzied discussion about what just happened, and the man at the counter pulled a small flask from his jacket and poured something into his coffee. Garrett couldn't blame him.

Nor could he take his eyes off Lana Burns. She went to her table and leaned back against the booth.

Why did she put herself at risk like that?

Anna suddenly blocked his line of vision. "Did you need cream and sugar?" she asked him.

"Sure," he said, then caught himself. "I mean, no, thanks. I take it black."

"It's gonna be a few minutes for the pancakes because of the distraction, but it'll be worth the wait."

"Thanks." A distraction? Is that what they called it?

Garrett got out of his booth and started for Lana's table, but Scooner and his friends beat him to it. Garrett wished he'd gotten there first. Scooner shifted next to her in the booth.

"I'm fine, go on." She shoved at Scooner's shoulder. "Stop hovering."

"I'll escort you home."

"Thanks, but I haven't eaten my pancakes yet and you guys are done with your meal."

"I've got this," Garrett said, shifting into the booth across from her. "I need to ask Miss Burns a few more questions anyway."

He held her gaze, trying to figure out if she was relieved or more irritated that yet another man was strong-arming his way into her protective services.

"And who are you?" one of Scooner's friends asked.

"He's the FBI agent I told you about," Scooner explained to his friend. "Agent Drake, this is Anderson Greene and Bill Roarke."

Garrett shook hands with the men.

Anderson wore wire-framed glasses and leaned on a cane, and Bill had jet-black hair, trimmed short, and a mustache and had a notebook tucked under his arm.

"If there's anything we can do to help with the case…" Anderson offered.

"Thanks, I appreciate that."

"For the record, I made sure Lana was safe in her apartment and figured she'd stay there for the night," Scooner said in apology.

Garrett glanced at Lana for an explanation.

"Mom called, worried sick about what happened so I had to go calm her down. Then I was too hyped up to sleep, so I took a walk and stopped in for some pancakes."

"Gentlemen, thanks for your concern, but I've really got this," Garrett said, hoping they'd take the hint.

Scooner didn't move at first. The kind of guy you definitely wanted on your side.

"I'll make sure she gets home safely," Garrett said.

"Good luck keeping her there." Scooner slipped out of the booth, and the men wandered out of the restaurant.

Garrett directed his attention to Lana, who looked oddly calm considering what just happened. "I'm not sure if I should be impressed or…"

"Or…?"

"Your interaction with Michael could have gone a completely different way."

"I suppose." She glanced out the front window and fingered a silver cross dangling from her necklace. He noticed her hand tremble slightly, probably from the adrenaline rush.

"Are you okay?" he asked.

She cracked a wry smile. "I'm fantastic."

"Miss Burns, I study human behavior for a living. Try again."

The handsome agent wasn't letting Lana off that easy. *Handsome? Really, Lana? After what happened to you, you're crushing on the enigmatic agent with the intense brown eyes?*

"Lana?" he prodded.

She stretched out her hands on the Formica table to ground herself. "For someone who found a dead body earlier tonight, and had to order pancakes while being threatened at knife-point, I'd say I'm doing pretty good."

"What made you do it? Talk to him like that?" he said, his voice softer than before.

"I couldn't risk him threatening someone else who'd pull a stupid move and get hurt. Like Scooner." She shuddered. "He means well, but that could have been a disaster."

"Let me get this straight. You put yourself in danger to protect a former navy SEAL, trained to do battle with the enemy?"

"Well, when you say it like that, I sound wacky."

"And you assumed you could talk the teenager out of stabbing you because…?"

"You said I had good instincts," she shot back.

With a frustrated shake of his head, he sipped his coffee.

Truth was, only now did she realize what could have happened. But Lana believed in the human spirit and the grace of God. She knew danger when she saw it, and Michael wasn't dangerous. He was desperate.

"Michael didn't want to hurt anyone," she offered. "He was hungry."

"And you knew this how?"

"I saw it in his eyes." She shrugged. "He made a bad decision, but we all deserve a second chance."

"You could have been seriously injured. Are you always this impulsive?"

"Impulsive, huh? I'll have to add that to the list. It's a long one depending on who you ask. If you asked my sister, she'd say I was disorganized, overly trusting and persuasive, bordering on manipulative, whereas the ex-boyfriend said I was controlling, too frugal and obstinate about the wrong things. At least in his opinion they were the wrong things."

She was rambling. She knew it. With Michael she'd kept talking to distract him from doing something he'd regret but now, well, the full weight of what had just happened twisted her stomach into knots.

"But then, what do ex-boyfriends know, right?" she continued. "He also thought I should stop giving tours, sell my snack shop and get a real job, you know, like working at a call center or selling insurance. I could go back to school I guess, but I've only got a few thousand in savings and—"

"Breathe," Agent Drake interrupted.

"What?"

"You're going to pass out if you don't take a breath. Am I making you nervous again? I could…" He motioned to get up.

"No." She automatically reached out, but her hand came up short of his fingers, looped through his coffee mug handle.

Anna delivered Lana's tea and glanced at the agent. "Oh, so you're over here now?"

Agent Drake hesitated before answering.

"Yes, he's joining me for dinner," Lana said.

"You mean breakfast?" Anna smiled.

"That, too."

"Pancakes should be out shortly." Anna winked and breezed off.

Truth was, Lana hated eating alone and since her breakup with Vincent, she'd been doing a lot of that lately. Flying solo.

Flying solo? You could have had your wings clipped, girl.

But Lana had to help Michael. She recognized something in the teen's eyes and it wasn't the desire to hurt anyone. She'd seen it in Sketch's eyes, her talented, seventeen-year-old computer assistant.

"I'm going with impressed," the agent suddenly said.

She eyed him. "What?"

"I'm impressed by how you handled that teenager."

"Wow, can I get a junior FBI badge or something?"

"Don't push it."

He looked surprised, like he hadn't meant to utter the playful retort. She thought he might have even cracked a smile but couldn't be sure. It would be a vast improvement on his permanent frown, his lips stretched into a thin, straight line.

"I'd like to ask a favor of you," he said.

"Sure."

"Promise me you'll never do that again?"

"You mean…"

"Insinuate yourself into a dangerous situation like that."

Lana dunked her tea bag in the hot water and sighed. He was asking the impossible. She couldn't turn her back on someone who was in so much pain they were blinded to the beauty of life and the grace of God. She knew how precious life was, and how short it could be.

"I'm sorry, I can't make that promise," she said.

"May I ask why?"

"You may ask."

"But you won't tell me, will you?"

She shrugged.

"Ignoring a direct order. You're definitely not getting that junior agent badge."

She smiled to herself at his unexpected response. He wasn't berating her for not answering; rather, he respected her space.

"Two orders of Boomer's blueberry pancakes." Anna slid a plate in front of Garrett, and a double order in front of Lana.

"Whoa, that's a lotta pancakes," Lana said.

"The hero of the evening gets a double order. On the house."

"I knew risking my life would pay off." She snapped her attention to Anna. "Sorry, that was a weird thing to say."

"It's okay." She touched her shoulder. "You've had a stressful night."

"Yeah, nothing like a plate of Boomer's to make it all better. Can I get a to-go box? I'm bringing half of this to Michael."

"That kid who—"

"Yep, that one." Lana stuck her fork into the pancakes and cut the pile in a perfect half. "Thanks," she said to her friend who hovered, probably dumb-founded that Lana was serious about bringing dinner to Michael.

"A to-go box. Check," Anna said.

Agent Drake slid the tray of syrups in front of Lana. "Can I try for another favor?"

"Sure." She squirted maple syrup on her half of the stack.

"Once I drop you off at home, can you promise not to go out again tonight?"

"Now *that,* I can do."

When her alarm went off the next morning at six-thirty, Lana didn't even bother hitting the snooze but-ton. She lowered the volume on a Jonny Diaz song and let the soulful timbre of his voice lull her back to sleep. Just for a little while. She'd earned it. She knew once she started her day the phone would ring nonstop with questions about last night's drama: a dead body, a teenager threatening a restaurant full of people…

A handsome FBI agent joining Lana for dinner, tak-ing her by the police station to drop off pancakes, then escorting her home. She didn't want to think about how *that* story was going to evolve by lunchtime.

There was no story, just a Federal agent doing his job. And last night he'd made it his job to get Lana home safely, to make sure she did not "encounter any more personal threats." His words.

During their meal he'd asked if she'd meet with a sketch artist to create an image of the man who'd tried to force his way onto the tour boat last night. Lana was pretty sure the guy was a pushy businessman used to getting his way. She'd encountered a few of those since she'd started Delightful Tours.

But she'd rarely encountered men like Agent Drake, sophisticated and imposing in his crisp dark suit, with intimidating eyes that challenged her whenever he glanced in her direction. He did the whole "brooding male" thing exceptionally well. Probably came with the job description.

Yet last night, after Lana talked a teenager out of stabbing her, the agent offered Lana a compassionate shoulder. He'd even teased her a few times. An image of his slight smile drifted across her thoughts....

She imagined sitting at the Turnstyle across the table from him, sharing a plate of pancakes, only this time he wore a knit shirt and jeans. His hair wasn't perfectly combed, rather it was mussed in front, and he had a sparkle in his eye....

Pounding made her jackknife in bed. Heart racing, she scanned her bedroom and realized she'd fallen into a deep sleep. She glanced at the clock. It read 7:14.

Persistent knocking echoed through her apartment. Someone was trying to wake her up.

She slipped on her robe, fastened it in front and hesitated at the front door. She checked the peephole and spotted Agent Drake hovering in her hallway. She stepped back. He knocked again. With a quick breath she opened the door.

"Good morning," she said, surprised to see him at her place so early.

"It's not too early, is it? I was able to get a sketch artist. He'll be here in half an hour." He cast a quick glance at her robe, then averted his eyes. "Sorry. Chief Wright said you're always up by seven."

"I usually am. Do you want to come in?"

"No, I'll wait by the car. I have to make some calls."

"Oh, okay. Give me twenty minutes."

"Take your time." He turned and went down the stairs.

"Hey, wait a second, isn't that the same suit you had on last night?"

He turned. "I was hoping you wouldn't notice."

"You mean you were up all night?"

"I'll be in the car."

"I'll bring coffee."

"Great, thanks."

She shut her door and rushed into the kitchen to put the coffee on. Talk about a man dedicated to his job. He hadn't slept? He was up all night? Doing what? You couldn't interview potential witnesses at three in the morning.

Whatever the reason, she felt safer knowing how determined he was to find whoever killed the man who'd washed up on Salish Island.

Lana showered and was dressed in fifteen minutes. She filled two travel mugs with coffee and pulled a couple of Mom's cranberry-nut scones from the freezer and defrosted them in the microwave. She bagged them, grabbed her purse and coffees and headed out.

When she opened the apartment building door, she spotted the agent's car across the street in the exact spot he'd parked it last night when he'd accompanied her upstairs.

Wait a sec, he couldn't have stayed there all night, could he? Watching her? He was taking a swig from a blue, reusable water bottle when she crossed the street and handed him a coffee. "This will wake you up faster than water."

"Thanks." He opened the car door and put it in the cup holder.

"Don't tell me you slept in your car last night."

"Okay, I won't." He went around the front of the sedan and opened the door for her.

"If you weren't a federal agent, I would be seriously creeped out."

"Then it's a good thing I'm a federal agent." He shut her door.

He was worried about her, his potential witness. Garrett probably figured Lana was his best lead on this case. As she shifted the bag of scones onto the console between them, she reminded herself his interest in her was strictly professional.

He got into the car and she motioned toward the bag. "I brought scones for breakfast."

"When did you have time to bake scones?"

She smiled. "I baked them in my sleep."

He raised an eyebrow.

"They're my mom's. She's always trying to outbake her friend Caroline, who owns the Port Whisper Inn."

His grip on the steering wheel tightened as he pulled away from the curb. "Thanks, I'll have mine when we get to the P.D."

"You didn't really sit outside my apartment all night, did you?"

"Not all night."

No, Garrett stopped by his former mother-in-law's place early this morning, hoping to get the awkward encounter over with. No one answered when he knocked, which seemed odd since she ran an inn out of her home. Maybe she didn't have any guests.

More likely she saw him from an upstairs window and chose not to open her door. He couldn't blame her. There was too much history there, too much pain.

"You okay?" Lana asked.

"Yep."

He'd be better once she gave a description to the sketch artist and Garrett could get traction on this case.

"I may not study people for a living, but I'm going to make an educated guess that you're really not okay," she said.

"I'm tracking a serial killer."

"No, it's something else."

How on earth was this woman able to read him so easily? Not good. Garrett prided himself on being able to keep the ugly corners of his mind private, hidden, even from his own team.

"I'm tired. Didn't get much sleep," he said.

"I'm sorry."

He cast her a sideways glance. "It's not your fault."

"You were sleeping in your car because of me."

"Partly, and partly because I didn't have time to get a room. So, how about loading up a scone on a napkin for me?" he said to divert her.

Truth was, he shouldn't have slept outside her place, but something was nagging at him. And not just her captivating golden-green eyes.

She reached into the bag and grabbed a scone with a pale blue napkin. When she handed it to him, his fingers brushed against her soft and delicate hand. He snapped up the scone and took a bite.

"You know where to turn?" she said.

He swallowed. "Yep."

"Is it too dry?"

"What?" He turned onto Third Street.

"The scone?"

"It's perfect."

Like the woman sitting next to him. Whoa, he was suffering from a serious case of sleep deprivation. Regardless that she seemed pretty perfect—strong, confident and beautiful—Garrett wasn't in the market, not now, nor in the foreseeable future. Not as long as he worked for the BAU.

She pulled out a scone for herself. As they drove through town, he realized they must look like a couple eating in companionable silence on their way to work. He placed his scone on the console and sipped his coffee.

"How long do you think the meeting with the sketch artist will take?" she asked.

"Depends on you, I guess. Why?"

"I'm supposed to take a tour group out to the island."

"I'm sorry, but you'll have to cancel your tours for a few days. It's still a crime scene."

"Oh, right. I'd better notify my customers." She pulled out her phone.

Was the killer scheduled to be on Lana's tour boat today? No, now Garrett was completely drifting off course. Red Hollow was about kidnapping, demanding ransom and killing very specific victims: aggressive, domineering men. He didn't randomly choose victims so there was no reason for Lana to be in personal danger.

Unless Red Hollow considered her a threat.

Garrett pulled into the police parking lot and spotted a familiar car. Georgia must have brought the sketch artist. Garrett hoped she left the rest of the team back in Tacoma to work the case. There was no reason to relocate to Port Whisper until they knew for sure they were dealing with Red Hollow.

As they approached the door, a teenage girl with flushed cheeks raced up to them. "Lana! He's gone. I've been texting all night, and he hasn't answered and—"

"Shhh, calm down, Ashley." She motioned to Garrett. "This is Agent Drake."

"Hi," Ashley croaked, turning her attention back to

Lana. "Sketch is missing and I'm afraid he did something stupid, like try to find out who killed that guy and—"

"Hold on, take a deep breath." Lana placed her hands on Ashley's shoulders and they both took a deep breath together, then another. "Okay, start from when you guys got home last night."

"We went to Sketch's house and my parents came over and talked with his gran about the dead guy. My dad said he heard that an FBI Agent named Drake was at the scene, and everyone started freaking out that the killer is local and his gran was really upset and Sketch said not to worry, that he'd protect her, and she, like, flipped out and ran upstairs. We left, but Sketch texted me later and said he was going to find the killer."

"How was he going to do that?" Garrett asked.

"I don't know. Go back to the scene? Check out security footage?"

"How could he get access to security footage?"

"He's a computer genius," Lana offered. "He can find anything, anywhere, online."

"In other words, he's a hacker," Garrett said.

"He's helped the local police with cases," Lana argued. "You can ask Morgan."

Great, what Garrett didn't need was a complication in the form of a meddling teenager. "I'm sorry, Ashley, but Lana needs to meet with a sketch artist for the murder case. She'll have to help you find your friend when she's done."

Lana squeezed the girl's hands. "Did you call his grandmother?"

"No one's answering."

"She goes for her morning walk around this time. Try her in half an hour, okay?"

The girl nodded, but still looked shaken.

"I'm sure he's fine," Lana said. "He probably fell asleep at the pier and that's why he isn't returning your texts. He's done that before, right?"

"I guess."

"Would you feel better if we said a quick prayer?" The teen nodded.

Lana held Ashley's hands and closed her eyes. Garrett automatically took a step back, afraid he'd somehow ruin the divine moment.

"Dear Lord, please keep watch over our friend, Sketch," Lana started. "He's a brave young man who deeply loves his family and wants to protect them. Help him avert danger and find his way back home to us. Amen."

Lana opened her eyes and shot Ashley a smile that warmed even Garrett's numb heart. "Keep the faith, sweetie. He'll be okay."

Ashley nodded and seemed to have calmed down. Too bad Garrett couldn't feel that kind of inner peace from a prayer. He escorted Lana into the police station and was greeted by Georgia and Chief Wright.

"Georgia, thanks for bringing the sketch artist," Garrett said.

"I figured we had to move fast." She eyed Lana. "Is this the witness?"

"Yes. Lana Burns, this is Agent Hunt," Garrett introduced.

"Nice to meet you," Lana said, then gave the chief a hug. "Hey, Morgan."

Georgia leaned toward Garrett. "Friendly town."

"He's married to her sister."

"Ah. People still do that, huh? Get married?" Georgia teased.

"That's what I hear."

But not Garrett, or Georgia, or anyone else in their line of work.

"Why don't you two sit over here?" Chief Wright led Lana and the forensic artist to a quiet corner.

"What do you want to do while she's working with him?" Georgia asked.

"Why don't you interview other passengers from last night's cruise? I'm going to stay with Lana."

"Lana?" Georgia raised an eyebrow at his use of her first name.

"That's her name," he shot back.

Georgia's expression faded. She was being coy, but Garrett wasn't in the mood for anything but finding a killer and getting out of town.

"I texted you contact information for tourists this morning."

"Yep, got it."

"It's nearly eight. Shouldn't be too early to question them."

"What about forensics?"

"They'll call when they have something."

"I'll check in later, then."

Garrett sensed she wanted to catch his eye, but he was focused on Lana. A part of him hoped she'd seen the killer; another part prayed she didn't because it would make her a target.

Prayed? Really, Garrett? You have no right to pray.

Garrett spent the next hour checking leads through emails and phone calls. Everything led to dead ends.

"Wow, that's really good," Lana said from across the room.

The sketch artist flipped the pad around so Garrett could see it. "I'll send this—"

The door swung open and a frantic woman rushed into the station. Not just any woman—Garrett's former mother-in-law, Caroline Ross. She rushed up to the chief, so upset she didn't even notice Garrett.

"Morgan, I can't find Sketch. He didn't come home last night and Ashley said he stopped texting around two, and she said he was going to—"

She spotted Garrett and froze. An eerie silence blanketed the room.

Garrett stood. "Hello, Caroline."

Her eyes welled with tears. "I can't talk to you right now." She motioned the chief outside.

"What was that about?" the sketch artist asked.

"She's upset because her grandson is missing," Lana offered.

"Her…grandson?" Garrett's heartbeat sped up. The room seemed to tip sideways.

"Yeah, Sketch is her grandson," Lana said.

It was the same nightmare that haunted his dreams for more than ten years, even after the serial killer was dead.

Only, this nightmare was real: his son was missing. Taken? Brutalized?

"You mean…Steven?" Garrett said, gripping the back of an office chair.

"How did you know his name?" Lana asked.

"Because he's my son."

THREE

If Lana reacted to Garrett's confession, Garrett didn't notice. He was out the door in seconds, looking for his former mother-in-law. He found Chief Wright trying to calm her down in the parking lot as she paced back and forth. Garrett hovered close by and listened, not wanting to further upset her.

"It's my fault," she said. "I shouldn't have let him see how worried I was."

"He's probably fine," Chief Wright offered. "He's a smart kid. Did he say where he was going or what he was going to do?"

"I was upstairs when he left. He didn't leave a note or send a text or…" Her lower lip quivered. "Say goodbye."

"Ashley might be able to help," Garrett offered, clicking into agent mode. He couldn't let the emotional thunderstorm cloud his ability to find his son.

"How do you know Ashley?" Caroline challenged.

"She was here earlier, worried about her boyfriend." He couldn't even say his son's name.

"Sketch, his name is Sketch," Caroline said.

"I'll get Ashley back here." Lana pressed numbers on her cell phone.

Caroline glared at Garrett, her eyes brimming with resentment, maybe even hatred.

"We'll find him, Caroline," Garrett said.

"Ashley's on her way," Lana said, pocketing her phone and studying Garrett.

"Everything okay, Chief?" Anderson Greene called from the street as he got out of his car.

"Fine, Anderson, thanks." The chief motioned to the group. "Let's take this inside."

They filed back into the station. Caroline stood as far away from Garrett as possible, yet Lana stayed close. Why? She had to think him a complete loser to have left his child the way he did. Did Caroline's friends even know that Sketch's real father was not Olivia's husband, Kurt?

"So, Ashley came by earlier because she hadn't heard from Sketch?" Chief Wright asked.

"Yes," Lana said.

"How long ago?"

"About an hour, I guess. But we—" she glanced at Garrett "—didn't think it was a crisis, I mean, he's disappeared before."

"Not the day after a dead body washes up on shore," Caroline said. "But that has to be a priority, right, Agent Drake? The killers are always the priority."

"Caroline, it's not his fault," Lana defended.

"Sure it is. It's in my grandson's DNA. He's hot-wired to put himself in danger, just like his father."

Chief Wright glanced at Garrett for an explanation.

"I'm the boy's biological father." Even though it felt like his insides were being shoved through a meat grinder, he spoke the words with as little emotion as possible. Emotion would paralyze his ability to find Steven.

"Where would he go? A friend's house?" Garrett asked.

"He has no friends," Caroline said, her voice flat, as if that, too, was Garrett's fault.

"Ashley said he was rambling about finding the killer and protecting his grandmother."

Caroline started up a frantic pace.

Garrett stepped in her path and caught her eye. "It's going to be okay. We will find him."

"Don't you dare make more promises you can't keep," she hissed.

She wandered to a chair and collapsed. Garrett took a deep breath through the pain lodged in his chest. She'd planted the knife firmly in his heart, where it belonged.

"I think we should—" Garrett caught himself and glanced at the chief. "I'm sorry, Chief, this is local jurisdiction and obviously I have a personal conflict."

"What conflict?" Caroline said. "It's not like you've spoken to your son in fourteen years."

Garrett felt the need to defend himself, especially to

Lana, but this was a private family matter. He didn't owe anyone an explanation but his son.

If he ever saw him again.

You're overreacting. Teenagers do stupid things like stay out all night.

"I'd appreciate your help, Agent Drake, although I am little surprised to hear that you're his father," Chief Wright said.

"We told him his real father was dead," Caroline said.

"Wow," Lana let slip.

Caroline glanced at her. "Olivia didn't want to confuse the boy. Besides, Garrett made no effort to reconnect after what he did to them."

"What did he do?" Lana asked.

Ashley burst into the police station and Garrett welcomed the reprieve.

"I checked the pier, and by the lighthouse," Ashley said, out of breath. "I can't find him and he's not answering his cell."

"Last night he told you he was going to find the killer?" Garrett asked.

"Yes."

"How was he going to do that?"

"Um…" She fiddled with her car keys.

Lana put her arm around Ashley's shoulder. "Come on, sweetie, they need your help."

Ashley looked at Garrett. "He said he was going to do some background on the dead guy, then uh…well, hack into the FBI's computer system to see what they had so far."

"I told him no more hacking," Chief Wright muttered.

Garrett glanced at Caroline. "Hacking?"

"He's a bright kid with too much time on his hands and no strong male figure in his life. Well, at least until Morgan stepped up," she said.

Garrett looked at the chief.

"I'm doing my best, but work doesn't leave much time for mentoring a high school dropout," he said.

This was getting worse by the second. A high school dropout? Hacker? Criminal?

Garrett shelved his disappointment and stopped himself from casting blame on Olivia and her husband. He didn't have time to go there, not if his son was in danger, and the truth was, Garrett was as much to blame since he'd abandoned the boy.

"The last text you got from him was when?" he asked Ashley.

"Around two."

"Write down his cell phone number for me."

Garrett called FBI IT specialist, Jonathan Sackett.

"Yes, Dynamic Drake, how can I help you today?" he answered.

"I need a trace. Here's the number." As Garrett read it to him, he realized how surreal this felt. Chasing a killer in the same town where his son was living? But why was he here? Olivia and her husband lived in Portland.

Georgia stepped into the office and glanced at the group, curious.

"A local boy is missing," Garrett explained. No one corrected him. No one told his fellow agent that *he* was the boy's father.

"Who is this guy?" Sackett asked.

"Why, what's wrong?"

"His signal is bouncing all over the place, like he doesn't want to be tracked. Is it Red Hollow?"

"It's a missing boy."

"I thought you were closing in on Red Hollow."

"Can you trace the phone or not?" Garrett heard the irritation in his voice.

"Can do, but it's gonna take a few. I'll call you back."

Garrett pocketed his phone and turned to the group.

"What?" Caroline said, stepping up to him. "You can't find him, can you?"

"Sackett will find him, but he needs some time."

"What if he doesn't have time?" Caroline gripped Garrett's suit jacket. "What if the killer found out Sketch was looking for him and, and…?"

"We've been tracking this guy for three months," Georgia said. "If we've been unable to find him, some kid surely can't."

Although he knew she was trying to make Caroline feel better, Garrett could tell her words had the opposite effect.

"He's not just *some kid*," Caroline croaked. "He's

smart and tenacious, and he even helped Chief Wright solve a murder case involving Lana's sister."

Lana nodded her confirmation, then caught Garrett's eye. She shared with him what could only be described as a pitiful smile, as if to say, *You poor thing, your life is crumbling around you.*

But it wasn't. Nothing had changed. He was still one of the top agents at the BAU. Just because his son was missing—

"I appreciate your situation, ma'am," Georgia said. "But our team is focused on finding a serial killer, not finding a teenager who hasn't even been missing twenty-four hours. Agent Drake, shouldn't we—"

"Georgia, distribute Lana's sketch to surrounding law enforcement agencies, then finish your interviews and check in with the forensics lab. If they can't move quick enough, we'll have to get it to Quantico."

"Yes, sir." She and the forensic artist went to the door. She opened it and glanced at Garrett. "Sir?"

"I'm staying to help them find the missing teenager."

"But—"

"Check in this afternoon."

With a slight, curious nod, she shut the door.

This was why few members of his unit had spouses or children. Close personal relationships tended to blur an agent's focus. Like it was blinding Garrett right now?

No, finding the teen could be directly related to the

Red Hollow case, especially if the boy threw himself into the path of a sadistic serial killer.

"Thank you," Caroline said.

He glanced into her pale blue eyes. Her genuine gratitude made him uncomfortable.

"It's my job," he said. His cell vibrated and he ripped it off his belt. "Sackett?"

"This kid is either insane, or brilliant or a little of both."

"And he's where, exactly?"

"I don't have an exactly, because the signal's dead, but I tracked text messages sent at 5:00 a.m. EST. According to my calculations, he was in a state park."

Garrett glanced at Chief Wright. "There's a state park around here?"

"Fort Richland, north side of town."

Garrett redirected his attention to Sackett. "Which area of the park?"

"The last text was sent from the northeast corner."

"Thanks." Garrett turned to the chief. "The last text came at around 2:00 a.m. from the northeast section of the park."

"Oh, the caves! He tracked the killer to the caves!" Ashley cried.

"We don't know that, Ashley," Lana said. "He likes to go there to think."

"In the middle of the night?" Caroline shot back.

"The chief and I will go to the park," Garrett directed. "Caroline, go to the house in case he shows up."

"No, I need to go with you," she argued.

"And what if he comes home? It's possible he fell asleep somewhere and he'll wander in, and no one will be there. Please, I might be bad at some things, but I'm really good at this."

Caroline nodded and glanced at Ashley. "Could you wait with me?"

"Sure." Ashley left with Caroline.

"Let's go," Lana said, grabbing her purse.

"Wait, you're not—"

"I spent most of my adolescence in those caves," she interrupted Garrett. "You'll find him quicker with me as your guide." She marched outside.

Chief Wright glanced at Morgan. "Obstinate, like her sister."

"So I've heard."

And today he was glad she was on his team.

Agent Drake was acting brave and strong, and all those things that men do when they're in crisis. But as they searched the park, Lana sensed he was on the brink of falling apart.

Gut instinct told her men like Garrett Drake did not fall apart, yet keeping all that inside could make him implode. She'd seen the same kind of behavior in her sister, working year after year with homeless teens, pushing back the gut-wrenching despair to a place where it couldn't hurt her. Denial was a dangerous thing, especially when sooner or later something forces that hidden place to be exposed, releasing all the fear and devastation in a powerful rush of emotion.

Lana hated to consider what that rush would look like for Agent Drake. Not only did he keep the violence and depravity of his job locked up tight, but he was probably suffering from an unhealthy dose of guilt for abandoning his son.

Sketch was his son. Remarkable. She wondered how Sketch was going to react to that bit of news when they found him.

And they would find him. God had special plans for Sketch. She knew this deep in her heart.

"Where to next?" Morgan asked her.

"There's a cave around this corner." But when they turned the corner they hit a wall of sand and rock.

"It's been a while since I was up here," she said. "The moisture must have collapsed part of this one."

Garrett clenched his jaw.

She touched his arm. "Come on, we've got two more caves to go."

Trying to keep her step confident and her tone hopeful, she led Morgan and Garrett across the rocky cliff side.

"Chief!" Scooner called. A handful of people hovered on the beach below. "We're here to help!"

"Where did they come from?" Garrett said, shocked.

"Small town," Morgan said. "They mean well."

"Why don't you have them check the boulders along the shoreline to the west, and the cave on the other side of those alder trees?" Garrett suggested.

Morgan called down instructions and the volunteers split up.

Lana guided Morgan and Agent Drake up the trail

and spotted some beer cans in the distance. "Looks like someone had a party last night."

"He drinks, too?"

"Who, Sketch?" Lana glanced at Garrett. From his expression she sensed he couldn't take one more piece of bad news. "No, drinking is not his thing. He wouldn't be hanging out here drinking with a bunch of kids."

"Why doesn't he have any friends?" he asked tentatively.

"He's not like other kids his age. He's—" she hesitated "—he's more mature."

"No kidding," Morgan muttered.

Garrett looked at her for an explanation.

"Sketch is responsible for Morgan finally getting up the courage to propose to my sister."

"Yeah, thanks to his guilt-tripping lecture about me being a self-centered jerk," Morgan said. "There aren't a lot of teenagers who'd say that to the police chief. But I'm glad he did."

Lana smiled, remembering the day Julie showed up at Lana's apartment with an engagement ring. It was a bittersweet moment for Lana, who worried she'd never find true love.

Lana toed a beer can out of the way. Her breath caught at the sight of Sketch's army jacket on the beach below.

"His jacket," she said. "Sketch!"

Garrett rushed toward the beach, practically stumbling down the uneven trail. Lana and Morgan followed, but they couldn't keep up. Garrett landed on the rocky beach and frantically whipped his head right, then left.

"Steven!" he cried and darted out of view.

"Morgan," she said, worried.

"Stay calm."

Morgan led her across the rocks and helped her step onto the beach. She glanced in Garrett's direction and spotted him on his knees next to a body. Morgan gripped her arm for support as they approached.

"Steven," Garrett croaked. "Steven, can you hear me?"

Sketch, wearing only his boxer shorts and socks, lay on his side clutching his knees to his chest in fetal position.

A sob ripped from the agent's chest as he pulled off his suit jacket and wrapped it around his son.

Morgan kneeled beside Sketch and pressed his fingers to his neck. "His pulse is strong. I'll call for an ambulance."

"It's okay," she said, touching Garrett's arm. "His pulse is strong."

Garrett's shoulders jerked as he fought back sobs of regret and grief.

"You guys find something?" one of the volunteers asked as a small group approached.

Morgan and Lana shared a glance. "I'm on it." Morgan redirected the group away from the scene.

"It's my fault. I'm so sorry, Steven," Garrett whispered.

"He won't answer if you call him that."

Garrett absently nodded, but didn't move. It was as if he feared touching Sketch would make his condition worse.

"Sketch, come on, buddy, open your eyes," Lana tried.

She brushed bangs off his forehead. "Place your hand on him so he feels grounded," she directed Garrett.

He didn't move. Tears spilled over onto his cheeks.

She grabbed Garrett's hand and positioned it on Sketch's shoulder.

"We're here, Sketch. You're okay," she said. "But Ashley's completely freaked and your grandmother's worried sick."

Morgan jogged up to them. "EMT should be here in ten. My deputy's clearing the scene."

"Please, Sketch," Garrett said. "Please open your eyes." He squeezed his shoulder.

Sketch blinked a few times and looked up at Lana, Garrett and Morgan.

"Hey, there he is," Lana said. "How are you doin', buddy?"

He started shivering and pulled Garrett's jacket tighter around his shoulders. "What…happened?"

He seemed disoriented, frightened.

"You're at the beach," Morgan said. "Do you remember how you got here?"

He glanced straight at Garrett.

Lana held her breath.

"Who…are you?" Sketch asked.

"I'm FBI Agent Garrett Drake."

"Why are you crying?"

"Allergies." He wiped his cheeks with his shirt-sleeve. "Can you answer the police chief? Tell us what happened? How did you end up out here, without your clothes?"

"My…" Sketch glanced down, then up again, his eyes filling with panic.

"It's okay," Lana said. "You're going to be okay. We called an ambulance."

"I don't need an ambulance. I just need my clothes. I need to go home."

"Not until you get checked out at the hospital," Morgan said.

"I don't need to go to the hospital!"

Lana studied his terrified expression. Something had happened, something traumatic.

"It's procedure," Garrett said.

Lana realized he'd successfully clicked into agent mode.

"I don't…care. I'm fine." Sketch stood, trembling. Lana reached out, but he glared at her hand. "I don't wanna go to the hospital, Morgan. Then everybody will know, everybody will…"

He paled and his eyes rolled back. Garrett caught him as he went down. "Come on," he said, carrying Sketch in his arms.

"You should wait for—"

"He stood on his own, he's obviously got no broken

bones. If the ambulance isn't there by the time I get to the top, I'll drive him myself."

Like a man with superpowers, more like adrenaline, the FBI agent carried his teenage son up the rocky trail as easily as if he were carrying an infant.

He may have abandoned his wife and child years ago, abandoned them for reasons Lana couldn't possibly imagine, but she knew in her heart that Garrett Drake loved his son.

"I don't want to talk about it." Steven rolled onto his side, his back to Garrett.

"Agent Drake?" The nurse stepped into the examining area and motioned for Garrett to leave.

His feet wouldn't move. He wasn't leaving his son again, not after what he'd just been through. Which was what? Not knowing was driving Garrett completely nuts.

"Sir, you're going to have to—"

"I'm not leaving. Call your administrator if you have to. I'll explain the situation." Garrett leaned against the wall, crossed his arms over his chest and stared at his son's back. The nurse disappeared.

"Your grandmother's on her way," Garrett said.

His son didn't respond.

A few minutes passed. He had to try again. "I'm sorry if I upset you. That was not my intent."

"Whatever. Just go away."

"I can't."

"Why not?"

*Because I won't risk you being hurt again, because
I never stopped loving you or worrying about you.*

Was now the time to tell Steven the truth?

"Hey, Sketch," Lana said, stepping around the corner. "I called Ashley."

"I don't want to see her."

If his son didn't want to see the one person he felt
closest to— Garrett fisted his hand and pushed away
from the wall. What did Red Hollow do to him?

Lana must have had the same thought because
worry creased her forehead. "Agent Drake, can I talk
to you for a minute?"

He hesitated before following her out of the examining area into the E.R. lobby.

"How's it going?" she asked.

Garrett shook his head and glanced at the floor.

"That bad?"

"Worse."

"Maybe I can help."

"No, I don't want him describing to you in detail
how a sadistic killer tortured him."

"Hey, hey," she squeezed his upper arm. "There's
no evidence of that."

"Nothing physical."

She grabbed his chin. No one ever touched Garrett.

"Knock it off," she said. "You're good at your job,
right?"

"Yes."

She released him. "Then do it. You know how people think. Sketch is a brilliant, insecure kid who was

trying to impress his girlfriend. Something happened out there, but you're not going to find out by demanding he tell you."

"What am I supposed to do?"

"What would you do in any other situation?"

"Get his family in there, but I don't really count."

"Maybe not yet. But what about Caroline or Ashley?"

"He said he doesn't want to see them. That concerns me."

"He's a guy and he was found in a vulnerable state. I get it. Make him feel strong again. If you do that, he'll probably open up to Ashley and maybe even to you."

"That's never gonna happen," he muttered.

"For whatever reason, you abandoned him when he was little and you're layered in so much guilt, and maybe it's deserved, I don't know. But what I do know is that your son needs you right now."

"I don't know how to be a father."

"Do you love him?"

"Of course I do."

"Then you know how to be a father. Get back in there. Be there for him."

"Okay, coach." He almost smiled. Not something he did often or easily.

As he approached his son, Lana's words echoed in his mind: *make him feel strong again.*

He positioned a chair so he was facing Steven's back. Garrett wanted it to be his son's idea to roll over and speak with him.

"I'm sorry," Garrett said. "I've been curt and rude, and my only excuse is that I'm worried." *I'm worried about you, son.* "We've been tracking this killer for about five months now, and I could really use your help, especially if he was the one who—"

"He wasn't."

Relief was quickly tempered by questions. Who stripped him down and left him on the beach? And why didn't he come home? All questions Garrett ached to ask him, but knew better.

"Can I show you something?" Garrett said.

"I guess." Steven rolled over.

Garrett fought back the rage at the sight of Steven's bruised eye and split lip, two things he hadn't noticed when he'd scooped him up off the beach. No, his brain had been paralyzed with adrenaline and the need to get him to the hospital. Good thing the ambulance was waiting for them when he reached the top.

"This is the latest victim." He flashed his PDA, a photo of Rick Washburn from a few months ago.

"I thought he was dead."

"He is."

"Where's *that* picture?"

"You want to see the photograph of a dead man?"

Steven nodded.

Garrett found a shot on his phone and held it up.

"He wasn't in the water long, was he?" his son asked.

"Why do you say that?"

"He doesn't look that bloated."

"You're a smart kid."

"Some call me a smart…never mind."

"So, will you help me with this case?"

Steven shrugged.

Well, it wasn't *no*.

"Last night when you stopped texting Ashley, what happened?" Garrett asked.

Steven turned away, ashamed. Garrett was losing him.

"You found a lead, didn't you, about the dead body?"

"I thought so, but…"

Garrett leaned back in the chair and waited. He would not push this young man. His son. At some point they were going to have to have *that* conversation, but not now, not while Steven was lying in a hospital bed trying to recover from an unimaginable trauma.

"You can't dump a body in the middle of Puget Sound without anyone noticing," Steven began. "So I triangulated the current and time of day the body was found. I figured the killer either dumped the body on the other side of Salish Island, or held him there and the guy escaped. The west side is for tourists and the east side is pretty rugged, but there's a slip where you could tie up a boat and either take your victim into the woods, or weigh him and drop him."

"You've given this a lot of thought."

"Gran was scared. I didn't want her worrying about some serial killer renting a room."

"I'll have Chief Wright take me to Salish to check

out your theory about the east side dock. Is that where you were going last night? Back to the island?"

Steven wrapped his arms around his stomach and rolled over.

"I'm sorry, I shouldn't have pushed." Garrett got up and came around the other side of the bed. He handed his son a business card. "But I could really use your help. When you're feeling better, if you think of anything else, send me a text, or call, okay?"

"Yeah."

"And one more favor? Can you lay off breaching government computer systems? I'm going to have a hard time explaining why I've enlisted the help of a seventeen-year-old hacker."

Sketch cracked a weak smile. Garrett turned to leave.

"They said they'd take me over to the island," Sketch said, his voice tight.

Garrett froze. "Who?"

"Pete Lonergan and his friends."

"But they didn't?" Garrett didn't turn around. He knew it would be more difficult for Steven to tell this story if he was looking into Garrett's eyes.

"They said their boat was tied up by the caves. They said—" he cleared his throat "—'Let's hang out before we hunt a serial killer.' I should have known they were mocking me."

Garrett kept quiet, waiting for him to continue.

"I think they put something in my drink," Steven

said. "I fell asleep. I don't remember anything else, like…if they did anything to me."

"The doctor said, physically, you're fine. They didn't hurt you other than some minor cuts and bruises."

But the psychological trauma would haunt him for months, maybe even years: the not knowing, the vulnerability, the disorientation when he woke up. Garrett wanted to find Pete and his friends and—

"Agent Drake?"

Garrett closed his eyes, his heart breaking at the sound of his son referring to him as *Agent,* not *Dad.*

"Yes?" He turned around.

"Did you find my laptop by the caves?"

"No, I'm sorry."

"Oh." He bunched the cotton blanket in his hand.

"I'll have Chief Wright bring Pete Lonergan and his friends in for questioning."

"No!" Steven pleaded. "Then everyone will know what they did to me. Just stay out of it."

Garrett put up his hands in a calming gesture. "It's okay, if that's how you want to play this, I'll respect your wishes. But you should report the computer as stolen in case it shows up somewhere."

Sketch relaxed into the pillow. "I guess."

"I'm sorry, I know how laptops become like a second brain," Garrett said.

"It's okay. Everything's password protected so they can't get into it. And even if they destroyed it, everything's backed up on my server."

"That was a good move."

Steven shrugged.

"In a few days, when you're feeling better, I'd like to come by and see what you've got." *And tell you the truth.*

"Yeah, that's cool."

Caroline breezed into the examining area. "I'm not sure that's such a good idea." She stood on the opposite side of the bed, arms crossed defiantly like a mama bear. Garrett was glad the boy had his grandmother in his life.

"Gran, I'm fine. The FBI needs my help."

"A word outside, Agent Drake?" She marched to the door.

"Good luck," Steven said.

"Am I going to need it?"

"Oh, yeah."

"Thanks."

Garrett followed Caroline into the lobby. Once safely away from his son, she spun on him. "What do you think you're doing?"

"Making sure my son's okay. What's the problem?"

"Involving him in your work, Garrett, really?"

"He's vulnerable and insecure. He needs to feel in control of something, so I told him I could use his help. I was trying to give him some control back."

"Shouldn't you be out there tracking down the serial killer who did this to him?"

"It wasn't the serial killer."

"What?"

"You know a kid named Pete Lonergan?"

"You mean kids did this?" she said in a hushed voice.

"Yes. Psychologically, well, it might be a while before he bounces back. You can expect nightmares, anxiety, erratic behavior."

"And what about Pete Lonergan and his gang?"

"Steven wants me to leave it alone."

"Garrett, no."

"He doesn't want his shame broadcast through the Port Whisper grapevine."

"*He* has nothing to be ashamed about."

"I agree. Give him a little time. I'll speak with Chief Wright about how to deal with that Lonergan kid."

"And what about your own kid, Garrett? What are your intentions?"

Garrett glanced at the door to the examining area. "I can't think about that right now."

"Of course not, work comes first."

"No, Caroline. Don't you understand? By pursuing the killer, Steven could have unknowingly put himself in danger. That's a risk I won't take. I need to close this case or at least be certain that the killer hasn't targeted him before I can think about anything else."

Caroline sighed. "Enough people know the truth about you and Sketch. This is a small town. I hope you plan to talk to him before he hears it from someone else."

"Why is Steven living with you?"

"He and his stepfather had issues." She ambled toward the E.R. and hesitated, glancing over her shoulder. "Do you think they'll release Sketch today?"

"It sounds like it."

"Then…come by around six for dinner." She disappeared into the examining area, and Lana wandered up to him.

"That sounded encouraging," she said.

He glanced at her in question.

"She invited you for dinner. That's good, right? The perfect opportunity to tell Sketch you're his dad?"

He wasn't sure how to answer. The thought of confessing what he'd done, that he'd abandoned Steven fourteen years ago, wasn't a pleasant one. At least now, Steven was talking to Garrett. What would happen when he found out the truth?

"Just so you know, Sketch never really connected with his stepdad, although I hear he's a nice guy," Lana offered.

Garrett eyed her. "How do you know so much about my son's relationships?"

"I pick up on things, Ashley tells me things. He's a great kid, but he's kinda lost. My sister says he needs a strong male figure in his life."

"I was hoping his stepfather would fill that role."

"Well, he didn't. So—" she hesitated and eyed him "—What are you going to do about it?"

Behind the E.R. door his son lay bruised and humiliated, covered in blankets. Garrett would give anything to be able to ease his pain and erase the fear from his mind. But he hadn't the first clue how to do that with his seventeen-year-old son, a virtual stranger.

His cell vibrated and he ripped it off his belt clip. He read the caller ID.

"Georgia, what have you got?" he answered.

"There's been another ransom demand."

FOUR

Agent Drake pocketed his phone. "Can you give me a ride back to Port Whisper?"

"Of course." Lana sensed he was rattled. "What is it?"

"He's taken another victim. This time in Olympia." His voice was flat, expressionless as he headed for the exit. "Which means he's probably moved on from Port Whisper." He stopped suddenly and glanced over his shoulder in the direction of his son.

Her breath caught at the pain she read in his eyes.

She touched his upper arm to ground him. "Steven's okay. Caroline won't let anything happen to him."

He still didn't move.

The sliding doors opened and Scooner jogged into the hospital. His timing couldn't have been better.

"Scooner," she called him over.

"I heard about Sketch. Is he okay? Where's Caroline?"

Lana always suspected Scooner was sweet on Caroline and this confirmed it.

"She's inside with Sketch," she said. "Can you make sure they get home? It sounds like they're going to release him in a few hours."

"Absolutely. What about you two?"

"My team needs me," Garrett said in a guilt-laden tone, his eyes glued to the examining room door.

"A new development?" Scooner asked.

"We've gotta go," Lana said. "I'll call you later. And don't be surprised if Mom stops by Caroline's with dinner tonight."

"Check." Scooner rushed into the hospital.

Lana unlocked the passenger door for Garrett.

"I was supposed to stop by Caroline's for dinner tonight." He snapped his gaze to Lana's. "I was going to tell Steven..."

"Don't think about that now. Let's get back so you can find this creep before he hurts anyone else."

With a slight nod he got into the car. She rushed around to the driver's side, watching her passenger through the front windshield. He stared out his window like the gears were locked and his brain shut down, like he'd forgotten why he'd come to Port Whisper in the first place: to find a killer.

Coming face-to-face with his estranged son after so many years was a shocker for sure, and it obviously jarred something loose in Garrett's emotional headspace.

She wanted to help him get back on track and tap

into his analytical self so he could find the criminal who was threatening their town.

Pulling out of the parking lot, she asked, "What did the ransom say?"

"I'm sorry, I can't share that information with a civilian."

Good, he was thinking like an agent again.

"Was Sketch helpful? Did he get a description of the killer?" she asked.

"He wasn't taken by the killer. Local kids terrorized him."

"Agent Drake, I'm so sorry."

"You know more about me and my family than my own team. I think it's about time you called me Garrett."

"Sure, okay." She wasn't comfortable referring to him by his first name since it felt more personal and less professional, and professional was safe, it made sense. She'd never get personally involved with a man like Garrett Drake, a powerful, tortured man who hunted killers for a living.

Get personally involved? What are you thinking about, girl?

"I offended you. I'm sorry," he said.

"What? No, you didn't."

"You got quiet just now. That's unusual for you."

It was a statement, not a question. In twelve hours this man had figured her out. She'd dated Vincent for eight months and he didn't have a clue she liked chocolate sprinkles on peppermint ice cream, or favored jasmine bath salts above the rest.

"Which kids hurt Sketch?" She redirected the conversation.

"Pete Lonergan and his buddies. You know them?"

"Little Petey."

"My son could have accidentally died thanks to little Petey," he snapped. He glanced out the passenger window. "Sorry. I didn't mean that to sound harsh."

"It's okay." She sighed. "You have to understand, Pete was a little guy growing up. They used to call him Shortie the Shrimp, and Squirt. Then he had this growth spurt in the tenth grade and all bets were off. My guess is the anger turned inward made Petey a lost and not-so-nice young man."

"Not so nice? Really? Not mean, or angry or a sadistic bully?"

"That's another way of saying it, sure."

"But not your way," he whispered, gazing out the window.

"I guess, my point is, bad people aren't born that way."

"Some people might argue that point."

"And I'd have to argue that through forgiveness miracles can happen."

"I don't have much experience with either of those things."

"That's a shame."

The car fell silent and she didn't engage him for a few minutes. Yet something told her that if he kept getting tangled up in his own guilt and regret, it would blur his ability to solve this case.

"God forgives," she said softly.

"I don't believe in God."

"He believes in you," she offered.

"Well, He shouldn't."

"Garrett." She hesitated. "Why did you abandon Sketch? Was it a bad marriage?"

"It wasn't the best, but that wasn't the primary reason." He leaned against the headrest. "You don't want to hear this."

"Yes, I really do."

"Why?"

"I think it will make you feel better to articulate it."

"You sound like a psychologist."

"I'll take that as a compliment." She gripped the steering wheel and focused on the road ahead.

"It was fourteen years ago. We were profiling a serial arsonist in Boston. We were so close to catching him…" His voice trailed off. "Then one night, I come home and my garage is on fire. Olivia and Steven were upstairs, asleep when it started. Fire investigators determined acetone was used as an accelerant, the same kind used by the serial arsonist. They could have been killed because of me."

"I'm so sorry."

"I had to keep my family safe so I put them in protective custody until we found the guy. I thought we were close, but it took us three years to finally catch him. By then Olivia had remarried, said it would be less confusing for Steven if he had one father, someone who could always be there. I think she was afraid he'd admire me and my work and try to follow in my footsteps or something."

"It seems like he did that anyway. He's really good at figuring out puzzles and helping police. My sister wouldn't be alive if it weren't for Sketch. But you didn't, I mean, you never visited him? Didn't you miss him?"

"Yes, of course. But after a while the pain becomes a part of you. For the record, I did go to see him. I'd watch him on the playground from across the street and went to some of his baseball games."

"Sketch played baseball?"

"When he was little. I think he stopped around the fifth grade. I'm not sure why."

"Kurt is an athlete. That was probably his idea."

"Steven looked like he was having a good time. His stepdad coached his team for a few years."

"Things look different from a distance than they do up close."

"You sure you're not a psychologist or a sage or something?"

"No, but I've carried my share of burdens. I lost my dad when I was twelve. There isn't a day that goes by that I don't miss him. Sketch probably feels that way about you."

"You can't miss what you've never had."

"Sure you can. You can miss the idea of it. He had a stepdad, but Sketch probably felt like he couldn't

compete with the little brother Olivia and Kurt had together. Sketch and Kurt have had problems these last
few years, which is why he's living with his grandmother. It was a great move, don't get me wrong, but
deep down Sketch probably feels abandoned by his
mom, too."

"I need to call in," he said, ending the conversation
and pulling out his cell phone.

She'd stepped over the line. Drat.

Lana, you have to know when to stop. But seeing
people in pain broke her heart, especially people with
so much to give. Sketch had a ton to give and the
thought of him and Garrett being reunited as father
and son made her heart soar.

"For the record," he said, staring at his phone, but
not making a call, "my intention wasn't to abandon
him, but to protect him."

"I know."

"And not just from a serial killer, but from having
a deadbeat father unable to give him what he needed.
Kurt made all his baseball games and parent-teacher
nights, and all he brought home from work was a pay-
check and stories about disgruntled customers at the
paint store."

"Uh-huh."

"It was the right thing to do."

"I'm not disagreeing with you, but you talk like this
story's over and it's not. I know your focus is on finding a serial killer, but after you close this case, what
happens then, Garrett?"

* * *

Lana definitely pushed too hard because she spent the next forty-five minutes listening to Garrett bark orders to agents, demand answers from his tech guy and argue with the forensics lab about expediting results. It was as if he didn't want to think about her question, and by focusing on the case, he didn't have to. It's what she'd wanted when they'd left the hospital. She'd wanted him to focus on putting his personal issues aside and finding a killer.

But once he'd confessed his story about abandoning his son in order to protect him, about watching him from afar, she ached for the man who so desperately loved his son. She was trying to help him see that there was always hope, that he and Sketch could reunite and have a relationship.

When the case did come to an end, she worried that Garrett would cut and run because he had some warped idea that he didn't deserve a second chance, that he was a loser father, overly committed to his work with nothing to offer his son.

The man's heart was weighed down with massive amounts of regret, yet Lana felt she owed it to Sketch to cut through Garrett's guilt and open his heart to the possibilities.

Sketch had a chance to get to know his real father, grow into adulthood with his father by his side. A chance Lana didn't have. She sighed at the thought of what a difficult kid she'd been, always pushing back, always fighting for attention any way she could get it. Lana couldn't compete with her perfect older sister, thanks to Lana's learning disability and Julie's overachieving tendencies, so Lana resorted to acting out, mouthing off and pushing boundaries, much like Sketch. But he didn't just crave attention; he craved love and acceptance.

She'd only met Sketch's mother twice, but Lana guessed she was devoted to her new husband, as she should be. If Olivia had been forced to choose between her son from a first marriage, and her new family, well…that was an impossible position to be in.

"My gut tells me the killer messed up with Washburn, so I'll take another look around for evidence. There's a small dock on the east side where a boat could pull up out of sight…. Uh-huh…. No, I'm headed straight to the island. I'll call the chief. You head back and work with the team."

He pocketed his phone.

"So, to the dock, then?" she asked.

"Yeah, thanks."

"I can take you to the island on the *Princess*."

"I'll have the police boat take me over. Besides, I've kept you away from your business long enough."

"Well, since the tours are temporarily canceled, I only have to worry about the snack shop." She pulled her compact Chevy into a parking spot.

"Listen, about this morning…" His voice trailed off.

Right, this morning, when he'd spotted his unconscious son on the beach and thought he'd been brutalized, Agent Drake had fallen apart. She guessed he'd never broken down in public before, especially not in front of strangers.

"I'm glad Sketch is okay," she said. "See you later?"

"Yep. Thanks." He shut the door and started for the pier.

She grabbed her backpack and went into the snack shop. A few tourists were hovering out front, reading the cruise schedule.

"Sorry, folks, we're not offering boat service to Salish today," she said, opening the door to Stone Soup. It was nearly ten and if she was going to serve sandwiches, she had to get going on her prep work. A few customers followed her inside.

"If you were on the list for this morning's tour, you should have received a phone call canceling tours for at least the next forty-eight hours," Lana said. "The restaurant will officially open a little late, at twelve-thirty, due to an emergency."

Lana's mom, Edith, marched into the shop and gave her a hug. "Sweetie, I was so worried."

"Sorry, Mom, just got back from the hospital."

"Julie's on her way."

"What? Why?"

"I guess she wanted to make sure you were okay."

"I'm fine, but Sketch…" Lana shook her head. "He's a wreck. I feel so bad for that kid."

"Did a serial killer really kidnap him and hang him from the lighthouse by his ankles?"

"What? No, it was Pete Lonergan and his buddies.

They didn't hang him, but they drugged him and left him practically naked on the beach."

"Lonergan," Mom repeated. "That boy is trouble."

"Yeah, well, he wasn't born that way. He learned it from being picked on."

"I suppose you're right."

"Want to help me prep for lunch?" Lana pulled out cantaloupe, blueberries and watermelon for a fruit salad.

"Sure. I thought you might be in a bind so I brought along two dozen homemade focaccia rolls."

"But—"

"I used Caroline's kitchen at the inn to avoid any health code issues."

"You're awesome."

"Don't you know it." Mom winked.

"I don't suppose you have any coffee?" a middle-aged woman asked.

"In about ten minutes," Lana said.

Lana's sister, Julie, breezed into the shop.

"Aren't you supposed to be at Horizon?" Lana asked. Julie loved her new job as a counselor for a teen facility on the outskirts of town.

"I brought some of the boys into town to work on Luther's shed. How are you, little sister?" Julie hugged Lana.

"Boy, you guys act like *I* was kidnapped."

"What happened?" Julie said. "Is Sketch okay?"

"Physically, yeah. It might take a while for him to recover emotionally."

"Lana?"

She glanced across the shop and spotted Garrett by the front door holding his water bottle. Tall and imposing, he definitely stuck out among the tourists in his dark suit and tie.

"Agent Drake, this is my mom, Edith Burns, and my sister, Julie Wright, the chief's wife."

They shook hands and a sense of pride washed over Lana. She was proud of her family, and proud to be able to introduce them to a man like Garrett.

"What's up?" Lana asked him. "I thought you were headed out to Salish."

"Apparently they had a police emergency and the boat's unavailable."

"It's not…" Lana gripped the counter, hoping it wasn't another dead body.

"No, it's not related to the case," he said, reading her mind. "A couple took a speedboat out on the Sound and the engine died halfway to Salish Island. I guess the message didn't get out that no one is allowed on the island until the investigation is over."

"With our grapevine, you'd think everyone would have heard that message loud and clear," Julie said.

"I don't suppose your offer to give me a ride out there is still open?" Garrett glanced at the kitchen area. "Never mind. You're trying to get ready for customers. I'll wait for the chief."

"No, I can probably do it. I'll close up for a couple hours and—"

"Is it dangerous?" Mom interrupted.

"No, ma'am," Garrett answered. "We think the killer has moved on from your town, but to be safe, Lana will stay on the boat while I take a look around."

"How long will you be?"

"Shouldn't take more than an hour."

"Go ahead, Lana," Mom said. "Julie will help me prep for lunch, right, sweetie?"

"Mom, Julie has to get back to work and I won't make you prep all by yourself."

"Actually, I don't have to pick up the boys until one so I've got hours to kill," Julie said. "Of course, I'll expect a free sandwich out of the deal."

"Take two." Lana hugged her sister.

He shouldn't be involving a civilian, but a new victim, Mark Stetsman, had been kidnapped last night and could still be alive. Garrett had to get to the island and check out the dock his son had mentioned for clues.

His son. Garrett tried to shove back the emotional fireworks that sparked when he thought about Steven, but failed miserably. There wasn't a place deep enough to put all that regret. He'd missed out on the best years of his son's life. He'd never get those back. Yet Lana thought he still had a chance at having some kind of relationship with Steven.

"Garrett?"

He glanced at Lana and realized she'd repeated his name a few times. She looked adorable in an electric-yellow flotation device over a bright pink windbreaker and baseball cap that read Captain.

"Do you carry that thing everywhere?" She nodded at his water bottle.

"The job can be all consuming. Sometimes we forget to eat or drink. I got dehydrated once and almost passed out trying to… Well, let's just say it wasn't a good time to be dehydrated."

"Right."

A few minutes passed as they closed in on the island. "Do you want to do a drive by?"

"Excuse me?"

"My boat's too big to tie up on that little dock on the east side, but I can swing by if you'd like."

"No, I'll need to see it up close."

"Then we'll have to tie up on the main dock and hike in." She steered toward the dock.

Puget Sound was crowded with boaters taking advantage of the pleasant fall weather. As they got closer, he scanned the island. Even if the killer was still in the area, he wouldn't be caught at the scene of one of his crimes. There was no real threat here, yet something felt…off.

"Can you tie us up?" She pulled close to the wooden dock.

He grabbed the rope, climbed out and wrapped it around the metal dock cleat.

She cut the engine and started to climb out.

"Where do you think you're going? I told your mom you were staying in the boat and I meant it."

"Do you think the serial killer is here, on this island, right now?"

"Highly unlikely."

"Then I'm coming with you."

"Lana," he protested, but she reached for his hand and he automatically offered it. Pulling her out of the boat, she leaned into him to get her balance. She glanced into his eyes, then pulled away, her cheeks flushed. Was she scared of him? No, that was definitely awareness that sparked between them.

It was incredibly inappropriate to be noticing things like that, he reminded himself, and in any other circumstance he'd be able to deny the attraction. He'd dated women, taken them out for dinner and kissed them good-night. But none had blushed at a simple touch, or seemed to understand him without asking a lot of questions.

Lana Burns wasn't just any woman. She was a gentle, compassionate, Christian woman. A woman who shouldn't be anywhere near the ugliness of Garrett's work.

"I'll try one more time. I'd rather you stay here," he said.

"Then I'll never make it back to open for lunch." She started walking.

"Sorry?" He followed.

"It will take you hours to find the dock Sketch is talking about. It's hidden at the bottom of a curvy trail. You'll get there quicker with my help. Don't worry,

I've got my pepper spray." She patted her backpack and smiled. "Come on."

He wasn't sure what threw him off more, the fact she carried pepper spray, or that playful smile. Most civilians would be hesitant, maybe even terrified, to go to a scene where a serial killer may have docked a boat. But not Lana. She marched across the island like she was going into battle and had all the ammunition she needed: a canister of pepper spray and plenty of attitude.

He caught up to her, not hard since he towered over her by about seven inches and his legs were longer. "You're not scared?"

"Of what?"

"Of what we'll find down there."

"Like another dead body? No."

"What if the killer—"

"You said he wouldn't be here."

"I said it was unlikely. That's no guarantee."

"True, but I have pepper spray and you have a firearm, so I think we're good."

He glanced ahead and the hair pricked on the back of his neck. He decided it was better that she stayed close where he could protect her.

"The trail starts on the south side of the island and winds its way up and back down," she explained.

"You've been down there before?"

She hesitated.

"Lana?"

"Yeah, when I was a kid." A sad smile played across her lips. "I ran away."

"Why?"

"My dad had just died, I had no friends—at least it seemed like I had no friends—and Mom and I were constantly fighting."

"And you came here because…?"

"I could think here, without my family hovering, without having to see the pitiful looks on people's faces."

She led him through a thick mass of pine trees, and they picked up a small trail.

"People were worried about you," he offered.

"I guess. Where'd you grow up?"

"Chicago area."

"Your folks still alive?"

She was chatting to be polite, to pass the time, he got it. But he wasn't in the habit of sharing personal information.

"Too personal, huh," she asked and answered. "Sorry, I forget that everyone's not like me. I'm pretty open."

"No kidding," he joked.

"Hey, I worked hard to get this way," she defended.

"I wasn't criticizing. I'm just not used to being around people like you."

"What, naive?"

"Utterly and completely open."

She didn't respond and he wondered if he'd offended her. Since she walked in front of him, he couldn't read her expression, which was usually a good barometer of what she was thinking and feeling.

"No! No! No!" a man's voice echoed up to them.

Garrett put his hand on Lana's shoulder and stepped around her. "You stay close to me, got it?"

She nodded, her golden-green eyes widening with fear. That was an expression he would have rather not seen.

As he slowly headed down the trail, he slipped his firearm from its holster. Clutching it with two hands, he pointed it toward the ground until he had something to aim at.

Red Hollow?

Not possible. That would be too easy.

"No! No! No!" the voice shouted again.

"How far?" Garrett asked Lana.

"Below those rocks."

He heard her shuffle around in her backpack, probably in search of her pepper spray. Naive? Hardly. This woman was prepared for the worst.

Garrett wouldn't let that happen.

They made the final turn and Garrett hesitated. "Stay back," he whispered.

Adrenaline pumping, Garrett slowly made his way down the trail past the last curve and dodged behind an evergreen for cover. He peeked around the tree and spotted a man lying on his side, clutching his ankle, a black camera bag on the dock beside him.

"Great," Garrett muttered. He marched toward the dock and scanned the surrounding area for signs of trouble. He had a pretty good idea what happened. Some photojournalist caught wind of Red Hollow striking in this small town and came to check it out.

"Aaahhh," the man moaned.

"Let me see your hands," Garrett ordered.

The guy stopped moaning and tentatively raised his hand. He looked at Garrett and he recognized the guy as Alan Brewster from the *Daily Press*.

"Agent Drake, help me," he groaned. "I think I broke my ankle."

Garrett holstered his firearm and motioned for Lana. "You shouldn't be here, Mr. Brewster."

"Don't I know it," he said.

"I'm going to have to confiscate your camera," Garrett said.

"Can you call an ambulance first?"

"I will, but it might be a while before they can respond." Garrett kneeled beside the photographer and took off the guy's shoe to check for swelling. "They only have one emergency boat and it's out on a call."

"Terrific."

"What happened?" Lana said, rushing up to them.

"I broke my ankle," Brewster said.

"Probably a bad sprain," Garrett corrected.

"What, you a doctor now?" Brewster barked. "Sorry, sorry."

"The first aid kit on the *Princess* has a cold pack and Ace bandages." Lana took off toward the trail. "I'll be back in ten!"

"Wait, Lana!"

"I'll be fine." She waved her pepper spray. "I'll call 9-1-1 to send a boat."

Garrett watched her sprint up the trail.

"So, my source was right? The killer was here, on this dock?"

Garrett redirected his attention to the photographer. "Who told you that?"

"Anonymous."

Garrett narrowed his eyes.

"Honest. I got a text last night about a dead body floating up on Salish Island. Called your press office, but after they dodged me for a few hours I figured it was true, and came to check it out."

"This is a crime scene."

"I didn't see any yellow tape."

Garrett stood and walked away.

"Sorry, I—"

Garrett put up his hand to silence him. "Did you look around before you sprained your ankle or did you just fall out of your boat?"

"I got some good shots. There's a cabin up there." He pointed. "I didn't see any furniture inside. Looks uninhabited."

"I'd like my tech guy to tap into your phone to see where the text came from. I'm guessing it's from the killer."

"Why would he do that?"

"He wants someone to tell his story."

Garrett walked slowly along the degenerating dock,

eyeing the murky waters below. Something in the water caught his eye.

Red.

Red rope. Braided rope.

He reached into the water and yanked it loose from the dock.

"What's that?" Brewster said.

"He was here," Garrett whispered. He snapped his gaze to the ridge above.

"Lana."

FIVE

Calm. He had to remain calm.

Not easy when panic surged through his veins, panic at the thought of the lovely Lana Burns being Red Hollow's next victim.

Garrett was halfway up the trail in seconds.

"What about me?" Brewster called after him.

"He needs you to tell his story. You're in no danger."

Garrett got to the top of the trail. He jogged west as he called Agent Hunt. "Georgia, it's Garrett. I'm on Salish Island. He's been here. I found red braided rope."

"Why are you out of breath?"

"Lana Burns is with me and I'm afraid for her safety."

"You brought a civilian—"

"I need you to get one of our forensics teams to the east side of the island ASAP."

"I doubt he's there. He's supposed to be at the ransom drop in an hour."

"He's never shown up before."

"But we know he's close. He likes to watch. Maybe we'll—"

"Georgia?"

Nothing. He must have dropped the call, stepped into a black hole or something. He didn't have time to stop and check how many bars he had.

Lana was alone, vulnerable to a sadistic killer because she wanted to get the first aid kit and help a stranger. That was Lana, always thinking about the other person before herself. Garrett figured that out pretty quick.

Garrett ran faster, angry with himself for involving her in this case. She was fragile, gentle and innocent, and he'd seen enough innocents brutalized in his line of work. He couldn't let anything happen to this special woman.

He spotted her boat in the distance, but no Lana. Calling out would be unwise because it would expose Garrett's location to Red Hollow.

His heartbeat skipped at the thought of the murderer stalking her, coming up behind her, slamming his arm around her throat and dragging her off.

Pushing the dark images aside, he jogged up to the dock, slipping his firearm from its holster. From this vantage point the boat was empty. But her body could be down, she could be unconscious on the floor. He crossed the wooden planks as quietly as possible.

Approached the boat.

Took a deep breath.

And spotted her bright pink windbreaker huddled in the corner.

"Lana?"

She popped up, aiming the pepper spray at him. She quickly lowered it. "Whoa, you almost got nailed there, buddy."

She eyed the gun in his hand, the muzzle pointed down. "Garrett, what happened?"

He filled his lungs with air, only then realizing he'd been holding his breath. Holstering his gun, he said, "I found evidence linking the killer to this island and I thought you might be in danger."

"No, I'm fine. What did you find?"

"I couldn't see you as I was running across the island—"

"I had to dig for the first aid kit."

"Or from the dock, and we would have passed if you were on the way back to help Brewster."

"Garrett?"

He looked into her golden-green eyes.

"I'm okay," she said.

He heard her words, but they didn't register. The adrenaline still rushed through his body, fueled by concern that he'd put her in danger.

His worst nightmare, the reason he shied away from personal relationships. He wouldn't put someone he cared about in danger ever again.

"We should get you back," he said.

"After we help Mr. Brewster, right?"

"Of course."

She grabbed the first aid kit, and he offered his hand to help her out of the boat. When their fingers touched, he noticed how small and delicate they felt in his hand. She stepped onto the dock and he hesitated before letting go. The way she looked into his eyes, with such trust, such admiration, drove him insane. He wanted to tell her he wasn't worthy of her admiration.

He wanted to tell her to stay as far away as possible.

"You okay?" she asked.

He released her hand and took the first aid kit. "Fine."

As they headed back to Brewster, Garrett admitted he was irritated at having to tend to the arrogant photographer. It was the man's own fault he was lying on the pier with a sprained ankle. That was Brewster. Always on the chase, always on the hunt for the next big story.

He and the serial killer had a lot in common in that regard. In a way, Garrett did, as well. But did Garrett have arrogant tendencies that could put civilians like Lana in danger? He couldn't be sure the killer wasn't on the island right now, watching them, laughing at Garrett as he raced across the island, fearing the worst had happened to Lana.

"Say something." Lana looked up at him with concern in her eyes.

"I'm sorry?"

"You're wound tighter than my sister, Julie, and she can get pretty twisted up. It's bad, isn't it, the evidence?"

Using the latex glove, Garrett pulled the piece of rope from his pocket. "Same type of rope the killer uses on his victims. I put a call into Agent Hunt to send one of our forensics teams out here to comb the island."

"What's happening with the latest victim?"

"The ransom drop is supposed to take place in an hour." He realized he shouldn't be talking to Lana about the case. It could only put her more at risk. "I owe you an apology."

"What for?" she said.

"I never should have asked you to bring me over today. I put you at risk and that's extremely unprofessional of me."

"I could have said no."

"But you didn't." He shot her a sideways glance. "Why?"

"You said you didn't think we'd be in any danger and I trusted you."

He snapped his gaze to the trail ahead. "Maybe you shouldn't have. After today I'm not sure I trust my own instincts."

"Okay, grumpy."

"You're being trite about this?"

"No, I'm trying to snap you out of it. Look, you're running on no sleep, you're tracking a killer and your son—who you haven't seen in fourteen years— goes missing. That's enough to make anyone a little grumpy."

"This is my job. I deal with this on a daily basis."

"The no-sleep and tracking-a-killer part, sure, but not the missing-son part. You've been through—you're still going through—a personal trauma. Stop being so hard on yourself."

"Still going through it? You think what happened with Sketch has affected my judgment?"

"Not at all. But you're planning to tell Sketch the truth, right?"

"Yes."

"So, your professional energy is being tapped to the max and telling Sketch is going to tap into your emotional energy. You've got some major trials ahead of you, my friend, and beating yourself up only makes you weaker and less able to do your job, both as an agent and as a father. Why do that to yourself?"

"You sure you don't have a degree in psychology?"

She smiled that enchanting smile that almost made him believe in the goodness of a person's soul. What was it about this woman? She spoke to him with raw honesty, like there were no social barriers between them. Given their diverse lives, he found that refreshing.

"Sorry." She sighed. "I'm sure *outspoken* is on my list of faults."

"I'm glad it is." As he said the words, he realized he'd rarely been so honest with another human being. In the last ten minutes, he'd had an intimate conversation with a woman who should be a stranger, but felt closer than that, closer than any family member or friend ever had.

Which only meant he was having some kind of emotional breakdown because you don't get this close with a stranger this quickly.

As they approached the dock, Alan Brewster waved them over in a panic. "I tried emergency, but got cut off and I heard a rustling sound up there and I didn't know where you were and I thought—"

"Slow down, Mr. Brewster. Everything's fine." Lana kneeled on the aged wooden planks and Garrett handed her the first aid kit.

"How do you know that? You can't know that. She can't know that," Brewster said to Garrett.

"She's right. Look." Garrett pointed across the water at an approaching police boat.

"See," she said, glancing over her shoulder at Garrett. "It's all going to be okay."

Lana Burns was an enigma. She had a gentle nature, yet exuded strength and confidence. She'd obviously seen her share of ugliness, like finding her father's dead body when she was a kid, yet she still exuded unwavering hope. He wasn't sure how she managed that combination, but it fascinated him. So much so, he'd sent her back to Port Whisper with the emergency boat, so she wouldn't be a distraction. He would have had a hard time focusing on the case if he was worrying about her being in the same vicinity as a killer.

It took the rest of the day for the forensics team to show up and do a thorough search. As they were finishing up processing the mystery cabin, Garrett's phone vibrated. For a quick second he hoped it was Lana calling to check up on him. *Whoa, buddy, where did that come from?*

"Drake," he answered.

"It's Georgia."

"He didn't show, did he?" Garrett knew if it was good news she would have called sooner.

"No, sir."

"He's playing with us. Where was Mark Stetsman last seen?"

"Barnes & Noble in Olympia. He was speaking about his book, *Being the Alpha Male Your Woman Needs*."

"Interview the staff and anyone you can track down who attended the lecture. Ask about strange interactions with fans, heated discussions, you know the drill."

"Yes, sir. Did they find anything else on the island?" Georgia asked.

"So far, nothing other than the red hollow rope."

"Well, it is a boating community."

"Meaning?"

"Never mind."

"Georgia?"

"There's no evidence that the killer stayed in Port Whisper after the murder. It's obvious to the rest of the team that Red Hollow's moved on."

"It's not obvious to me. I'm staying here until we're sure he's no longer a threat. You continue to work the case from Tacoma."

"Without our team leader?"

"When I'm gone, you're in charge. So lead, Agent Hunt. I'll be in touch tomorrow."

Garrett ended the call, more than a bit frustrated, both with the lack of evidence found on the island today and with her lack of faith in his instincts. Yet didn't he just tell Lana she shouldn't trust his instincts because they could have put her in danger?

"We found something in the cabin." A tech walked up to Garrett holding an evidence bag. "Looks like the button off a man's dress shirt. We'll see if it matches the buttons on the victim's shirt." The agent headed toward the boat.

Garrett started to follow him, but the hair pricked on the back of his neck. He squinted, spying into the thick mass of trees on the north side of the island. The killer wouldn't be so bold as to stalk Garrett, would he?

Garrett found himself heading up the trail, away from the forensic techs. Fear didn't hold him back; it energized him. He quickened his pace and followed the trail past towering pine and cedar trees. A soft crack drew his attention to the left.

He withdrew his firearm. Held it close. Headed in the direction of the sound. The buzz of silence rang in his ears as he closed his eyes and listened. His fingers shifted around the butt of the gun.

"Drake!" a tech shouted.

Garrett focused on a small clearing between the trees, trying to make out—

"Agent Drake!"

They were packed up and ready to go. Garrett could tell them to wait…

No, he was being paranoid. So desperate to nail Red Hollow, he was seeing danger where there was none.

He shoved his gun back in place and marched to the dock.

I'm so close I can see the worry lines creasing Agent Drake's forehead. I thrill at the sight of his angry frown and the determined set to his lips.

I am just as determined.

Nothing will prevent me from fulfilling my duty and ridding the world of worthless bullies, not even the hard-edged, arrogant agent.

"I need to soften those edges," I whisper as I watch the boat leave the island.

Yes, I will play with his mind, like a cat stalks a mouse, catching him and batting him around for entertainment. Sending the team on a wild-goose chase this morning was a delightful diversion.

They'll never find Mark Stetsman. Not until I want them to.

"Careful," I remind myself. I can't afford to catch a case of arrogance from the sharply-dressed Agent Drake. I must stay humble and aware, which allows me to see things others don't.

Like the agent's attraction to Port Whisper's father-less, forlorn child.

"Aim for the heart of your prey," Teddy used to say. The old man knew where his stepson's heart was, con-

stantly poking at it with a blade or a knife or a shard of glass. The old man who didn't deserve to have a wonderful stepdaughter like Dianna.

This was all for her and others like her, oppressed by heartless bullies.

Agent Drake was a bully. But was he heartless? There was one way to tell, by taunting him, poking at him.

And I know exactly where to point my stick.

Helpless, yet determined. That's how Lana felt when she'd pulled away from Salish this morning. Garrett had sent her back to Port Whisper to run her business, while he stayed behind to do a search of the cabin for evidence that the serial killer had, in fact, been there.

As she wiped down the prep table, she shuddered at the thought of a serial killer being in the same zip code. She'd been careful not to let Garrett see her trepidation. She suspected any hint of fear would drive him away, and he needed someone positive like Lana in his life, at least until he healed his relationship with Sketch. She hoped she could be the conduit between father and son, the person who would help them see that love and forgiveness could conquer even the most paralyzing resentments.

Her sister and Morgan were proof of such grace touching the lives of estranged high school sweethearts, bringing them back together in the glory of love. Years of hurt and resentments could not keep them apart when they'd found each other again through forgiveness.

She only hoped Sketch could bring himself to forgive Garrett when he discovered the truth. And Garrett? She longed to ease his pain. He held himself to such a high level of performance that he was bound to fail.

She knew the feeling, seeing failure every time you looked in the mirror, blaming yourself for everything bad that happened in your life. After Dad had died, she'd blamed herself for the fight they'd had only days before the heart attack that took his life.

But being surrounded by the love and support of family and friends kept her from falling headlong into the abyss. Their love and her first mission trip, when she was nineteen, brought Lana out of her dark hole and opened her heart to God. Through his love she found forgiveness and the path to grace. She'd been at peace ever since.

That is, in everything but her love life. Would she ever find a man who'd accept her for who she was, nervous rambling and all?

"You have to have faith," she whispered to herself.

She flipped chairs onto tables and glanced at the clock. It was nearly seven. She usually closed at four but stayed open into the dinner hour to recoup lost income due to the canceled tours. She looked forward to heading home, slipping into her pajamas and relaxing with a good mystery novel.

But even then she knew she wouldn't stop thinking

about Garrett. He needed to tell his son the truth, and soon, especially since too many people knew, and it was hard not to keep that kind of secret confidential.

She flipped the last chair, took a sip of her iced mocha and started sweeping the shop. Someone tapped on the front door. She glanced up and spotted her mom smiling through the glass.

"Hey," Lana said, opening the door. "I thought you were taking dinner to Caroline's tonight?"

"Just dropped it off."

Mom followed Lana as she went in back to fill the water bucket to mop the floor.

"Aren't you leaving soon?" Mom asked.

"After I mop and scrub sinks. You want a mocha, or herbal tea or something?"

"No, thanks. Let me help you with closing chores."

"Uh, no, you've done enough today. Thanks again for prepping this morning." Lana planted her hands on Mom's shoulders and placed her in a nearby chair. "It won't take me long."

Lana squirted bleach cleanser in the sink and scrubbed. "How's Sketch?"

"Hiding out in his room. I was hoping Caroline would convince him to come out after I left. I don't think he wants to be around people right now."

"Poor kid."

"I never got a chance to ask… What happened on the island this morning?"

"A lot of drama." Lana cocked a half smile. "We

found an injured photojournalist on the east dock. Other than that, nothing."

The last thing she needed was Mom overreacting about Lana being in danger. Lana knew as long as Garrett was close by, she'd be safe.

"What do you make of that Agent Drake?" Mom asked. "Did you know he's Sketch's biological father?"

"Yep."

"I don't understand how he could leave his son like that, just abandon him."

"We'd understand if we had walked in his shoes." She winked at her mom. "Which we haven't."

"I don't mean to be judgmental."

Lana rinsed the sinks. "I wasn't accusing you of being judgmental. You're curious. It's an understandable question, especially since we love that kid so much."

"I don't suppose the agent talked about it. Sketch, I mean?"

"He did, in confidence." She assumed he wouldn't want her sharing personal conversations with others, even her mom.

Garrett seemed to trust her, something she guessed was unusual for the reserved agent. She would respect that gift.

"You like him," Mom said matter-of-factly.

"We all like him."

"Not Sketch, that FBI agent."

"He's a complicated but good man." Lana grabbed the mop.

"Who hunts killers for a living."

"That's true."

"All over the country."

"Yep." Lana glanced at her mom, whose face had gone white.

"Mom, what's wrong?"

"I don't want to see you hurt."

"What are you talking about?"

"First Gregory in high school, then Vincent and now this FBI agent."

"Whoa, whoa, whoa. Mom, Garrett's in town to solve a murder. He's not here to date the locals."

Mom glanced at the floor, and Lana hugged her. "Oh, I love you for worrying about me so much."

"It's just…after we nearly lost Julie last year, I thought I was done with the threats to my daughters' lives. Now there's a dead body and a serial killer and you like an FBI agent who hunts killers for a living and abandoned a wonderful boy like Sketch when he was only three."

Lana stroked her mom's back to get her to stop her frantic ramble. "Shhh. It's okay. I'm not in danger. The killer's probably long gone. Now come on, I'm sending you home." Lana guided her toward the door.

"You sure you don't need my help?"

"You know how you can help me?" Lana smiled. "Go home, watch reruns of *I Love Lucy* and relax. Okay?"

"How did you get to be such a mature young woman?"

"I have a great mom."

"Well, don't be surprised if your great sister stops by to check up on you. Call me when you get home?"

"Will do." Lana sent her on her way.

With a sigh, she grabbed the mop. She'd work faster if she could focus on closing duties, as opposed to chatting with Mom or Julie about Sketch's situation, the dead body that washed up on Salish Island, or the agent assigned to find his killer.

Garrett. She wondered how he was doing. By midafternoon she'd caught herself glancing up every time the door cracked open, thinking it might be him, back in town and needing sustenance. But he'd probably had his fill of chatterbox Lana and picked up a burger down the street.

Just like Lana needed to focus on her business, Garrett needed to focus on this case. He didn't need her distracting him with a gazillion questions, or offering suggestions on how to connect with his son.

She wrung out the mop and glanced at the wall clock. It was well past seven. Had he gone to the Port Whisper Inn to speak with Sketch? Would Caroline even let him in?

Lana wished she could be there to help Caroline, Sketch and Garrett mend their relationship and get their family back on track. She folded her hands together and said a silent prayer for Garrett, a man being pulled in two different directions by his job and his family.

She finished mopping and realized she had yet to inventory the walk-in refrigerator to make sure they weren't running low on something critical for tomorrow's customers.

She flipped on the light switch and stepped inside. As she scanned the shelves she noticed she was short on whipping cream, greens and roast turkey.

The door slammed shut behind her.

She spun around and grabbed the handle, but it wouldn't budge.

The light went off, plunging her into complete darkness.

SIX

He never felt more exposed in his life, or more vulnerable.

As Garrett stood on the front porch of his former mother-in-law's inn, he searched his brain for the right words, and he searched his heart for courage. He needed words to explain why he'd left his son and courage to knock on the door.

He cleared his throat, clutched the bouquet of flowers, his peace offering, tightly in his hand, and wished Lana was standing beside him.

He'd cruised by her snack shop twenty minutes ago and saw that the lights were still on. He figured she'd stayed open longer than usual to try and make up for lost revenue from canceled boat tours. He didn't want to make her day longer by asking her to get involved in his personal drama.

This wasn't simply drama. It was his life, possibly his future.

Now he was being ridiculous. Even if his son forgave him, there was no room in Garrett's life for a teenager. Garrett worked twelve- to sixteen-hour days. A boy needed attention, needed his dad to be around.

But Lana was right. Too many locals knew the truth. Garrett was not a coward. He wouldn't let Steven find out from a stranger.

With a confident fist, Garrett knocked. Waited. Knocked again. He paced a few feet away and back to the door. He took a deep breath to calm the adrenaline rushing through his body.

The front door cracked open. Caroline looked exhausted, worried and tense.

"I'm sorry I'm late," he apologized. "We had a situation."

"So did we, Garrett."

"What happened? Is Steven—"

"He's hiding in his bedroom."

"Probably sleeping off the medication," Garrett said. "That's to be expected."

"If you say so."

"I'm sorry I missed dinner."

"We all missed dinner. Sketch wouldn't eat. I couldn't eat because I've been so worried about him."

"He's a tough kid, Caroline."

"Just like his father?" She quirked a brow.

"That's not what I meant." He offered her the flowers.

She sighed and planted her hands on her hips. "I'm tired, Garrett."

He lowered the flowers in defeat. "I understand."

"I don't. I don't understand any of this."

Silence stretched between them. With a nod, Garrett turned to leave. He didn't want to upset her more than he already had.

"Garrett, stop. I'm sorry, please come in." She swung open the door and led him down the front hallway into the kitchen. He sat at the aged wooden table and she stopped, studying him.

"What?" he said.

"That's Sketch's favorite seat."

Facing the door with a good view of the window. Could he have inherited Garrett's instincts?

Caroline filled a vase with water. "Thank you for the flowers."

"It's the least I can do for someone who's raising my son."

"He's a good boy, just a little too smart for his own good."

"Yeah, so he said."

"Did you get dinner?" she asked.

"No time. I can grab something at the Turnstyle."

"Nonsense, I'll warm up some chicken." She pulled a casserole dish out of the refrigerator and filled a plate with chicken and mashed potatoes.

"It was the right thing to do," he said.

"What?"

"Sending them away."

"For who, Garrett? For you, because you needed the career boost and you couldn't concentrate with a wife and young son around the house?"

"Caroline, you know that's not true. A killer was after me."

"But even after you caught him, you never reached out to your son."

"Olivia asked me not to." Garrett sighed. "You also know Olivia and I were having issues long before I sent them away."

"Yes, I'm aware." Her voice softened. She put the plate in the microwave. "Maybe you could have solved the issues if you'd stayed together, I don't know." Her pale blue eyes sparkled with unshed tears. "But I do know that boy upstairs has suffered, Garrett. He's suffered because of your decision."

"And I'll spend the rest of my life trying to make it up to him."

"How will you do that, Garrett? You're leaving town once your case is solved, right?"

Garrett didn't answer. He couldn't.

"I thought so." She slid the plate in front of him and sat down.

"It's my job," he defended.

"And Sketch is your son."

"I didn't come here to argue with you, Caroline."

"I know, I'm…" She hesitated. "There's been so much to deal with today and the phone's been ringing off the hook. People want to know what's going on."

"What have you told them?"

"That Sketch was terrorized by kids, but didn't see who they were."

"He asked you to keep their names out of it?"

"Yes." She sighed. "I'm really worried. He never spends time in his bedroom and he hasn't been in the command center since he's been home."

"The command center?"

"The basement. He has all kinds of computers and gadgets down there. It's his passion. It...was his passion."

"He'll be okay. Just give him a few days." Garrett took a bite of chicken. It tasted amazing. "Wow."

"Edith Burns brought it over, you know, Lana's mother?" She quirked a brow.

"Why are you looking at me like that?" He took another bite.

"Rumors have started. I know I have no right to ask, but Lana's a sweet girl and I'd hate to see her hurt."

"So, stay away so I don't ruin her life, too?"

"I didn't say that."

"You didn't have to."

"Garrett—"

"It's fine. I get it. I wouldn't want me dating my best friend's daughter, either." He glanced at his watch, needing a sudden escape. The whole conversation about staying away from Lana had killed his appetite.

He stood. "I'll stop by tomorrow to talk to Sketch, if that's okay. Maybe around noon? He should be up by then, right?"

"Garrett, I'm sorry if I—"

"Caroline, it's fine. I need to check on something. Tomorrow, then?" He strode down the front hall, not waiting for her response.

"Okay, sure."

He went outside and hesitated on the porch, eyeing the misty rain. His gut was tangled in knots over not being able to help his emotionally bruised son, and being drawn to Lana despite anyone's warnings to stay away, including his own.

At this point he felt like he had little control over his personal life, so he'd throw himself into the job, like always.

Regardless of warnings or common sense, he needed to thank Lana for taking him out to the island. The detour had obviously put her behind at work.

He'd stop by Stone Soup and help her close, if she was still there. Then he'd escort her to her apartment across the street, and say his final goodbye.

He was getting pressure from his team to join them and there was no compelling evidence to keep him here. He'd speak with Sketch and head back to Tacoma.

It was the right thing to do.

He drove into town, hoping Lana would understand his decision to leave. Then again, maybe she didn't feel the unexplainable pull between them and wouldn't care. He knew she'd ended a relationship recently, so she'd probably surrounded herself with emotional barriers to keep anyone from getting close. The last thing on her mind was to dive into another relationship, especially with a total stranger.

Now what was he thinking about? A relationship? *Really, Garrett?*

The lack of sleep these past few days was messing with his cognitive function. Maybe tonight he'd get a good night's sleep. Thanks to Chief Wright, Garrett had secured a room above Bill Roarke's restaurant down the street. The eatery closed at nine so it shouldn't be too loud.

After his conversation with Caroline, there was no way Garrett would ask to stay at her inn. It would be too painful for her, and if the reunion between Garrett and Steven went south, well, that would be emotionally stressful, on top of trying to solve a murder case.

He pulled up in front of Stone Soup and noticed the lights on.

Garrett approached the front door and turned the handle. Locked. He tapped a few times on the glass. Nothing. Peering inside, he called her cell phone. Something caught his eye. Her phone had fallen off the counter and vibrated across the floor.

He rushed to the back of the snack shop, but that door was locked, as well. Calling the police chief's private number, Garrett rushed back to the front of the building. Maybe she was fine and had forgotten her cell phone at work.

But she wouldn't have left the lights on.

Garrett's call to the chief went to voice mail. "Chief, it's Garrett Drake. Sorry to bother you, but I'm trying to find Lana. I'm here at the snack shop, it's locked up tight, but her phone's inside and the lights are on. Call me."

He shoved his phone into his pocket and fought the frantic beat of his heart. He felt frustrated and helpless.

And responsible. If anything happened to her...

He analyzed the lock, trying to figure out how to break in without completely ruining the door. He pulled out his gun and aimed the butt at a small pane of glass, one of nine that made up the upper half of the door.

"Agent Drake?" Lana's sister, Julie said, coming up behind him. "What's going on?"

"I need to get inside. Do you have a key?"

She adjusted her hood for protection against the rain. "No, sorry, Mom does. Want me to—"

"No time. Please step back."

Her eyes widened as she realized the severity of the situation. With a quick jerk, he broke the glass, reached through and unlocked the door.

"Lana!" he called, more of a demand than a question.

"Lana?" she said, rushing into the back storage area.

A muted thud echoed across the shop. "Lana, do it again!"

Three taps reverberated from a large, silver door.

"The cooler," Julie said, scrambling to grab the handle. She tugged but couldn't get it open.

"Let me." Garrett gripped it with both hands and yanked. "It's jammed. Does she have tools?"

"In the back."

"Find me a crowbar or something to leverage it open."

Julie darted around the corner.

"Lana! We're going to get you out of there! Can you hear me?"

One thump against the door.

Julie rushed around the corner. "Here." She handed him a long screwdriver.

Garrett leveraged it against the door handle, clenched his jaw and jerked. Once. Nothing. Twice. Nothing. On the third try the door sprang open and Julie tumbled out. He scooped her up into his arms and carried her to a small sofa up front where customers waited for to-go orders.

He tried to step away and let Lana's sister get close, but Lana wouldn't release his arm. Her fingers pinched his skin as she searched his eyes. She was trying to tell him something.

"Lana, Lana sweetie, what happened?" Julie asked.

"D-d-d-door j-j-j-jammed. C-c-cold. Can you... g-g-g-et me tea?"

"Absolutely." Julie rushed into the kitchen area.

Garrett ripped a colorful blanket off the back of the sofa and wrapped it around her.

"It didn't jam, did it?" Garrett said in a low voice.

"D-d-don't know. Light...went off. Locked in."

The fear in her eyes sent a new surge of panic through Garrett's chest. Was he responsible for what happened because he'd involved her in the case?

He couldn't think about that now. He rubbed her arms, hoping the friction would get the circulation flowing in her body.

"We should take you to the hospital," he said.

"No, want to g-g-go home."

Bill Roarke, owner of the building, and his buddy Anderson Greene came into the shop. "What happened?"

"She got locked in the cooler and I had to break in," Garrett said, but he wasn't looking at the men. He was studying Lana's eyes, eyes that pleaded not to say what they both feared: that this incident was related to the Red Hollow case.

Lana probably didn't want to worry her family. He could understand that, but he would not walk away from his responsibility to protect her.

"Hot tea," Julie said, trying to edge Garrett out of the way.

He didn't take it personally. She probably knew the sordid story about Garrett abandoning Sketch, and it was clear how Caroline felt about Lana developing feelings for Garrett.

The whole town could be against him, but it didn't matter. His goal was to keep her safe. Well, that, and find Red Hollow.

Garrett shifted aside, but Lana wouldn't let go of his hand. He glanced over his shoulder at Bill and Anderson. "You got here awfully quick."

"My beeper goes off if the silent alarm triggers in any of my buildings," Bill said. "Anderson and I were having coffee at the Turnstyle."

"Great, the whole town probably knows I locked myself in the cooler," Lana said.

"Hey, you're talking without a stutter." Julie offered

her the mug of hot tea and glanced at Garrett. "Do you think we should take her to the hospital?"

"Already tried that."

"At least have Doc Saunders check you out," Julie said.

"I'm fine. Just embarrassed, and tired and still cold." She sipped tea.

"This is gonna cost me," Bill said, analyzing the broken pane of glass.

"I'll cover it," Garrett said.

"Nah, I wouldn't want to—"

"I insist." Garrett wandered to the cooler and analyzed the door. They could dust for prints, but if it was Red Hollow that would be a waste of time. He never left prints.

He flicked the light switch and the bulb popped on. But when he'd opened the door it was pitch-black in there, which meant...

Someone had been standing right beside the cooler with his finger on the switch. He was inches from Lana.

"Did you figure it out?" Anderson said.

Garrett snapped his attention to him. "What?"

"Why the lock jammed? I have some experience with locks. Worked at my dad's shop growing up."

"By all means, take a stab at it." Garrett stepped aside and puzzled over how the intruder got into the shop and left without breaking any locks or doors.

There was only one explanation: he had a key.

Garrett eyed Bill Roarke, who was still analyzing

the front door. Once Garrett got Lana settled he'd call in a background check on Bill.

"It's missing something, like a pin," Anderson said. "The one thing that makes everything fit."

"Is it typical for those things to randomly fall out?"

"Not typical but it could happen. Why? What are you thinking?" Anderson studied him through wire-trimmed glasses.

The guy was looking for a scoop to add to the rumor mill.

"I'm thinking we've all had a busy twenty-four hours."

Across the shop, Lana raised her voice at her sister. "I said, no hospital." Lana stood and wavered.

"I'd better get Lana home." He nodded at Anderson. "Thanks for the help."

"Sure thing."

"Bill, see to things here?" Garrett scooped up Lana into his arms.

"No problem," Bill said.

"Wait," Lana said. "Jules, my phone's around here somewhere—"

"On the floor by the fireplace." Garrett nodded.

"And can you grab my backpack from the kitchen?" Lana asked.

"Sure." Julie dashed off.

Garrett carried her out of the restaurant.

"I can walk, ya know."

"Yeah, but then I wouldn't get my exercise for the day."

He studied a group of people hovering outside a restaurant up the street. One by one they turned to gawk at Garrett, holding Lana in his arms.

"Got everything," Julie said. She eyed their audience as they crossed the street. "The grapevine's gonna be buzzing tonight."

Lana didn't care what anyone thought or what kind of gossip burned the phone lines. She appreciated Garrett's gesture more than he could know. She didn't feel uncomfortable or awkward in his arms.

She felt safe.

As he carried her across the street, she struggled to let go of the anxiety knotting her stomach. She'd been locked in the cooler for what felt like hours, but she knew now it was more like twenty minutes.

Questions still taunted her. Was it intentional? Did someone lock her inside the cooler and turn off the light to frighten her? Had she become a target?

She studied Garrett as they approached her building. His eyes darted up and down the sidewalk, assessing possible threats. She needed to talk to him. Alone. How on earth was she going to make that happen?

They paused outside Lana's apartment building.

"Key?" Julie asked.

"Key chain in side pocket of my backpack."

Julie found the key and unlocked the door. Once they got to the second floor, Julie opened the apartment door and Lana hoped she hadn't left the place in a shambles. The door swung open and she breathed a sigh of relief.

"You okay?" Garrett asked, crossing the room and placing her gently on the sofa.

"She's probably relieved the place isn't a mess," Julie offered, shutting and locking the door. "I've got this, Agent Drake, if you want to take off."

"No," Lana said to her sister. "I'd prefer that he stayed for a while." She glanced at Garrett. "If you wouldn't mind."

"Not at all. I'll get you some water." Garrett went into the kitchen.

Julie shot Lana a what-is-going-on face and Lana waved her off. But her sister sat beside her on the couch. "You two seem awfully chummy."

"He's a nice guy," Lana whispered.

"Who hunts serial killers."

"So?"

"I know that look. Watch yourself, little sister. You said you weren't going to get involved for a while."

"We're not involved, not like that. It's professional."

"And I'm Cleopatra."

Garrett wandered back into the room with a glass of water and a small box of fudge mints. "I found these on the counter and figured... well, my mom used to give me chocolate to cheer me up."

"Thanks." Lana took the box and shared a tender smile with him.

"I'm calling Doc Saunders," Julie said.

"I'm fine."

"You're not acting fine." She stood and paced to the kitchen.

Her sister was right on one count. Lana had promised herself not to get emotionally involved with a man for at least a year after her breakup with Vince, and it had only been four months.

Although she told herself she and Garrett weren't getting involved like that, she also admitted she enjoyed spending time with him, relying on his strength and hoping he'd benefit from some of her wisdom.

She had to stop kidding herself. She was trying to heal Garrett, like she tried to heal Vincent, who always saw the glass as half-empty.

Lana had a tendency to want to heal people. She'd floundered in that dark place herself and pulled herself out shortly after her first mission trip. Working with less fortunate kids and families put her life in perspective and lightened her heavy heart. She loved the feeling and desperately wanted to continue helping others, especially if it meant pulling them out of self-inflicted misery. But how was she going to convince Garrett to forgive himself for sending his son away?

"I'm glad she's calling the doctor. You're too quiet," Garrett said, shifting awkwardly onto a bright yellow futon.

She couldn't help but smile.

"What?" He adjusted himself, but still looked incredibly uncomfortable.

"I don't have the best furniture for tall men."

"It's more comfortable than what I have to deal with on a commercial airplane."

"I can imagine."

"Lana, that look you gave me before at the restaurant." He hesitated. "Is there more to this story than you accidentally being locked in the cooler?"

Lana slipped the glass of water onto the end table. "Maybe, I don't know. The lock has been acting up for a while."

"Did you walk into a dark cooler without turning on the light switch?"

She snapped her gaze to his. "It was on, Garrett. I know it was. Do you think it was him?"

"Doc will be here in twenty minutes," Julie interrupted, sauntering out of the kitchen. "And I called Morgan, too, so there's really no reason for Agent Drake to hang around. Her family will take care of her."

"Julie, you're being rude," Lana said.

"Why? I figure he's got more pressing issues to deal with, like finding a serial killer, right? I mean, so my sister got stuck in the cooler. It happens."

Lana knew Julie was more worried than she was letting on, but she made no secret of the fact she wanted Garrett out of Lana's apartment and out of her life.

"She's right," Lana said. "I wouldn't want to keep you from your investigation."

Lana's phone rang in the kitchen.

"I'll get it," Julie said.

Garrett leaned close. "Lana, let's be clear. You are

part of my investigation. If there's any chance tonight's incident is related to—"

"Lana," Julie said, coming into the living with the cordless phone in her hand. "It's Mom."

"I've got to make a call anyway." Garrett stood. "I'll be right outside the door."

He left and Lana took a deep breath. "Hey, Mom."

"Julie told me. You got locked in the cooler?"

"Yeah, but I'm okay."

"I'm coming over."

"Mom, I'm fine. Julie's here, Agent Drake is here and Morgan's on the way. I just want to sleep, okay?"

"If you're sure."

"I am."

"Prove it and stop by for scones in the morning."

"Sure thing. Love you."

"You, too, honey."

Lana hung up and tipped her head back against the sofa.

Julie plopped down next to her. "I'm staying over."

"You don't have to."

"I want to. Maybe you should move back in with Mom."

"No can do."

"But you love Mom."

"It has nothing to do with love, Jules. I need to be my own person, which means being independent, not making my bed if I don't want to, or eating coconut cream pie for breakfast and Boomer's pancakes for dinner."

"How do you stay so slim eating all those carbs?" she joked.

"Look, you moved away and lived on your own for ten years. I'm twenty-seven, a grown woman. You and Mom need to respect my space and my decisions."

"Sweetie." She took Lana's hand. "We don't mean to be smothering or whatever. It's just, well, we worry about you."

"Because I was a wreck of a teenager, I get it. But the more you try to control my life, or help me make the right decisions, the more I get the message you think I'm incapable of taking care of myself."

"No, that's not—"

"That's how it feels. Jules, I hate to break it to you, but the only way I'm going to learn my own life lessons and grow as a person is to make mistakes. I need to fall down in order to learn how to get up again. I fell down with Vince, and I'm up. And if anything were to happen between Garrett and I, I'd have to learn that lesson on my own, as well. Have faith that I'll come out of it okay."

Julie leaned forward and hugged her. "Fine, I'll back off. You hungry? I could whip up a grilled cheese sandwich."

"Sounds perfect."

As she went into the kitchen, Lana pulled the blanket tighter around her shoulders. She kept up a strong front to Julie's face, but tonight's incident had rattled her. Getting locked in the cooler could have been a fluke, but the light going out?

Garrett came back into the apartment wearing a grim expression.

"What's wrong?" Lana asked.

Julie popped her head out of the kitchen.

"I've gotta go." He glanced at Julie. "Are you staying a while?"

"All night."

"Good. Please keep the door locked. I'll check in first thing tomorrow."

"Garrett?" Lana questioned.

"I'm sorry I have to leave so abruptly. Good night."

But it wasn't good. His mood had darkened and he avoided making eye contact. Who had he spoken to on the phone?

He shut the door with a click.

"He's not your problem, little sister."

"Jules," Lana said in warning.

"Sorry, sorry. Okay, so cheddar and Muenster or straight cheddar?"

"How about cheddar, Colby and Monterey Jack?"

"Whoa, you are high maintenance tonight." With a wink, Julie dashed back into the kitchen.

Lana turned around to look out her window. She eyed Garrett's car, parked across the street in front of Stone Soup. But she didn't see Garrett.

"What's goin' on?" she whispered.

Then he came into view, paced to his car and leaned against it. He was talking to someone on the phone, and from his body language she could tell he was extremely frustrated. He ran his hand through his dark hair, paced to the front of her shop, then back to the car.

"What kind of tea?" Julie called from the kitchen. "Jasmine or Earl Grey?"

"Jasmine, please," Lana answered, but didn't take her eyes off Garrett.

He suddenly stopped and glanced up at her window. She ducked like she'd been caught doing something naughty, a knee-jerk reaction. But she wasn't doing anything wrong. She was worried about him, and a little worried about her own safety.

Her cell phone vibrated on the table beside her. She recognized Garrett's number.

"Hello?"

"I see you spying on me," Garrett said.

She popped up and spotted him hovering under a streetlight, taking a swig from his water bottle.

"Busted," she said.

"Are you okay?"

"Yeah, just worried about you. You look stressed."

"You want to ease my stress? Shut your blinds and enjoy the evening with your sister. After the doctor checks you out, go right to sleep. Morgan and I will take turns watching your apartment to give you peace of mind, okay?"

"You think it was him, don't you?"

"I'm not thinking anything yet. But I'll guarantee you one thing. I'm not going to let anything happen to you."

* * *

Morgan relieved Garrett at three in the morning, giving Garrett the chance to sneak in a few hours of sleep in the room he'd rented above Bill Roarke's restaurant. The tech got back to Garrett, clearing Bill as a suspect. But then who had let themselves into the restaurant and terrorized Lana?

Garrett slept surprisingly well considering the call he'd received from Georgia last night pressuring him to rejoin his team back in Tacoma. Garrett couldn't leave, not when he feared the killer was still in town and had locked Lana in the cooler last night.

He rolled out of bed, showered and got dressed. If the killer had targeted Lana, Garrett needed to figure out how to protect her. He'd convinced Georgia to run things and give Garrett twenty-four hours to wrap things up in Port Whisper.

"Twenty-four hours. Yeah, how are you gonna do that?" he said into the mirror as he knotted his tie.

He had more than a murder case to deal with in Port Whisper. He thought about Steven, about him hiding in his room, about Caroline's accusation. *He's suffered because of your decision.*

She'd challenged him on his promise to make it up to him, and she was justified in doing so. How would Garrett make up fourteen years of absence when he traveled all the time, chasing down killers? His work was his life. It had been the only thing left after he'd sent his family away.

"Can't think about that," he muttered, walking to

Lana's apartment a block and a half away. He swung by the Magic Bean and picked up two coffees, a fancy one with whipped cream for her, and a black coffee for Garrett.

He glanced up the street but didn't see Morgan's cruiser parked outside her house. "Where are you, Chief?"

As he approached her building, an elderly woman opened the door. "Oh, Agent Drake, good morning."

"Good morning." He didn't remember meeting her.

"I'm Gretchen, Lana's neighbor. We all heard about her being locked in the freezer for three hours last night."

The town grapevine had been hard at work. He wondered what they were saying about him.

"Actually, it was the refrigerator and only about twenty minutes," he corrected.

"Well, that's a relief."

"Could you...?" He nodded toward the door.

"Don't bother making the climb. Lana's gone."

Garrett tried not to crush the cups in his hands. "Gone, where?"

"To her mother's. She left you a note. I happened to glance at it when I passed. Hope you don't mind."

"Do you—"

"It's 509 Oak Street. Take Cherry north two blocks to Edlund and make a right, then three streets over—"

"I'll find it, thanks." Garrett went to his car, put the coffees in the cup holders and punched the address into his GPS.

He pulled away from the curb a little too fast, anxious to get to the house. Why did Morgan let her out of his sight? They'd agreed that one of them would stay close to keep an eye on her.

He took a sip of coffee, hoping to clear the panic from his brain so he could focus.

Minutes later he pulled into the Burns's driveway behind three other cars including the chief's Jeep. Okay, so the chief was with her. Tension eased in his chest.

He grabbed the coffees and headed to the house. As he was about to tap on the door with his boot, it swung open.

"You'd better come inside." Lana opened the screen door. "One of those for me?"

He handed her the drink.

"Thanks," she said with a conciliatory smile.

"Lana?"

"They're all in back."

He followed her down the long hallway to the kitchen and hesitated in the doorway. Julie, Morgan, Anderson Greene, Scooner and a woman he assumed to be Lana's mother hovered around a distraught Caroline sitting at the kitchen table. She stared blindly into her teacup.

"What happened?" He slid his coffee cup onto the counter next to him.

"He heard you last night," Caroline said.

"Who heard me?"

"Your son." She glared at him. "And now he's gone for good."

SEVEN

The blood drained from Garrett's face. Lana touched his arm for support, but he didn't seem to notice.

"What do you mean, gone?" he said.

"Just what I said, Garrett," Caroline snapped. "He's gone and he doesn't want any part of this family or this town."

"Did he take your car? I can put out an APB on the plates," Garrett offered.

"Right, and arrest your own son. No, he didn't take my car."

"Which means he hitched," Lana said.

Caroline fiddled with her teacup. "I hope he makes his way back home to Portland."

"He won't go there," Lana offered.

Everyone looked at her, including Garrett.

"He blames his mom for abandoning him in Port Whisper."

"Don't be ridiculous, Lana," her mother said, stroking Caroline's back. "He loves his grandmother. It was his choice to stay."

"Of course he loves his grandmother. But deep down he feels like he can't do anything right, that he's a burden to the people around him."

"That's not what he said in his note," Caroline said.

"May I see it?" Garrett asked.

Caroline slid it across the weathered oak table. Lana picked it up and passed it to Garrett. He went outside onto the front porch and Lana followed.

She'd read the note and knew it would hit Garrett hard in the chest. As he absorbed the words, words written by a young man who felt utterly betrayed by people who were supposed to love him, Garrett absently leaned against the porch railing.

"He's right, everyone did lie to him." His gaze drifted across the front yard.

"You were going to tell him the truth," she offered.

"But I didn't. And now he's alone, angry and vulnerable." He motioned to the note. "He wrote, the other kids hate him, his family doesn't trust him with the truth, and he doesn't belong." He glanced into her eyes. "Anywhere. It sounds like he's thinking about—"

"Stop. You need to shut down those father feelings for a few minutes and think like an FBI agent on a missing-persons case."

He eyed the note in his hand.

"Agent Drake?"

He glanced up.

"A missing teenager—how would you find him?"

"Question the last person who talked to him, his family," he paused. "Friends."

"Let's start in the kitchen." She took his hand and pulled him back into the house. Maybe it was forward on her part, but it didn't feel that way. Garrett was temporarily blinded by worry and regret, neither of which would help them find Sketch.

"When was the last time anyone saw Sketch?" Lana asked.

"When I brought dinner over last night," her mom said.

"When I stopped by to question him about the kids who bullied him," Morgan offered.

"When I tucked him in," Caroline whispered.

A dull silence blanketed the room. Garrett squeezed her hand and only then did she realize she hadn't let go. He released her and passed the note back to Caroline.

"I need to speak with his girlfriend."

"I already called her. She's on her way over." Lana knew Ashley could help them figure out where Sketch went.

"Caroline, did you call Olivia?"

"No, not yet. Oh, Garrett, it's all my fault."

Garrett motioned for Scooner, who sat next to Caroline, to move and Garrett sat beside her. "This is not your fault. Olivia and I should have told him the truth years ago."

The front door flew open and Ashley raced into the kitchen. "I can't believe he left me."

Lana put her arm around her. "We'll find him."

"You don't get it. He doesn't want to be found."

She whipped out her phone and read a text. "Everyone lied to me. I can't trust anybody, not even Gram. I'm not even sure I can trust you." Ashley looked at Lana with tears in her eyes. "Why wouldn't he trust me? I love him."

"Is that all he said?" Garrett pressed.

"He wrote 'Don't look for me. Tell my Fed dad not to look for me. I want nothing to do with any of those liars.' But I never lied to him. You've gotta find him," she pleaded with Garrett.

"I know we're all worried, but he's a smart kid," Garrett said. "He's angry and hurt right now, but when he cools off he'll probably give his grandma a call or come back to town." He paused. "At least to take a swing at me."

"I feel so helpless," Caroline said.

"We're going to find him and he's going to be okay," Garrett assured. He stood and motioned for Ashley. "Can I have a word in private out front?"

"Sure."

Lana led Ashley to the porch.

"Caroline, stay off the phone in case he calls," Garrett said and followed them.

Lana and Ashley sat in the Adirondack chairs on the porch. Garrett crossed his arms over his chest and leaned against the porch railing.

"Ashley, you probably know him best. If anyone can help me find him, you can."

She sniffled. "Why did he leave me?"

"He's hurt," Garrett said. "When we're hurt our instinct is to run away from the pain."

"I didn't cause him pain."

"He's not thinking clearly right now or he never would have left such a special girl behind," Garrett said.

Lana didn't think a man was capable of speaking so tenderly to a teenage girl. Garrett glanced at Lana and her breath caught. Buried beneath layers of numbing armor, armor needed to see gruesome crimes day after day, was a sensitive, caring man.

"Ashley, can you tell us where he hangs out?"

"Besides my house and his command center? Mostly espresso shops that have Wi-Fi." She leaned forward as if not wanting anyone inside to hear what she was about to say. "He gets roped into doing chores for the inn and sometimes doesn't want to, so he'll disappear. There's one in Port Ludington he especially likes. It's got his favorite drink, hot chocolate with peppermint." She smiled. "He takes the bus and hangs out all day."

"Port Ludington is, what, an hour from here?" Garrett asked. "Why so far away?"

"The kids don't know him there, they don't, you know…"

"Tease him?" Lana offered.

Ashley shrugged. "He used to hang out at the Magic Bean until some guys waited for him to leave one afternoon and shoved ladies' hand lotion in his hair. It was gross."

"I'm surprised Chief Wright hasn't done anything to stop the bullying," Garrett said.

"Sketch asked him not to get involved. Sketch and the chief are kind of friends."

Morgan had been a much-needed father figure for Sketch. Garrett would have to thank him for that.

"Okay, so the place in Port Ludington, what's it called?" Garrett asked.

"Café Amour."

"Can you think of anyplace else he would go? Lana doesn't think he'd go back to Portland to see his mom."

"She's right. He'll barely talk to her when she calls the inn."

"Thanks. Lana, tell Morgan I'm headed to Port Ludington to check out this coffee shop."

"I'm coming with you."

"No, you have a restaurant to open."

"This takes priority. Ashley, tell them where we went and to call my cell if Sketch comes back."

"I want to come," Ashley protested.

"I need you to stay here in case Steven returns," Garrett said. "No matter what he's saying right now, he needs you."

"Okay, sure," the teenager said.

Garrett stepped off the porch and Lana followed.

"I can't talk you out of coming with me, can I?" he said.

"Nope."

"Want me to drive?" she offered.

"No sense using your gas." They got in his car and she studied him.

"You're calmer now," she said as they pulled out of the driveway.

"Thanks to your lecture. You were right, letting my emotions cloud my judgment is a disservice to my son."

"He'll be okay," she said, folding her fingers together in prayer. She closed her eyes and took a calming breath.

"You okay?" he said.

"Saying a little prayer for Sketch."

"Oh, sorry."

"Why?" She opened her eyes. "You should try it sometime."

He cracked a sardonic smile. "God stopped listening to me a long time ago."

"I doubt that."

"The eternal optimist."

"Is that a bad thing?" she countered.

He cast a quick, regretful glance in Lana's direction. "No, not at all."

They headed for the coffee shop where he hoped Steven was hiding out. "Would you mind telling me about my son?"

"I'd love to."

Forty-five minutes later they pulled into the parking lot behind Café Amour.

"I'm nervous," Garrett confessed, turning off the

ignition. He couldn't believe he'd uttered the words, but somehow, when he was in this woman's company, he didn't feel the need to cover up his feelings with alpha male attitude.

"It will be okay," Lana said. "He's a good kid with a big heart."

They got out of the car and headed for the coffee shop. Adrenaline pumping, he searched his mind for the right words in case he came face-to-face with his son. The alternative sent Garrett down a completely different road. If Sketch wasn't here…

Garrett hesitated as he reached for the door. The pressure of Lana's hand against his back stopped his spin of panic. He glanced down into her golden eyes. "Thanks."

"Sure."

With a sigh, Garrett opened the door and motioned for Lana to enter first. She glanced over her shoulder at him and smiled. "He's here. You want me to talk to him first?"

"No, let me give it a try."

"You got it, but one suggestion? Don't call him Steven."

"Roger that." Garrett and Lana approached Steven's table. The kid was completely focused on the computer screen, oblivious to their presence.

"Sketch?" Garrett said.

His son glanced up with a blank expression, like his mind was still absorbed in HTML code. Then he snapped back to reality and clenched his jaw. So, this was what Steven looked like when he was angry.

"What do you want?" Sketch said.

"To know that you're okay."

"I'm fine. Leave." He refocused on the screen.

"What are you doing?" Garrett nodded toward the computer.

"Looking for a tech job."

"Find anything good?"

Sketch hesitated, as if debating on whether to continue playing this game. Curiosity sparkled in his hazel eyes. "A few, but they all want degrees. I couldn't even get through high school. How am I supposed to get a bachelor's degree?"

"Start with a GED, then community college," Lana offered, and glanced at Garrett. "Sorry."

"Don't be." He redirected his attention to his son. "She's right, buddy. You've got the intelligence for school."

"Yeah, like you know anything about me." Sketch shook his head.

"I could use a coffee," Lana said. "You want something, Sketch? Hot chocolate?"

"Triple shot latte, lots of foam."

Garrett turned to go with her. Lana touched his arm. "I've got this. Coffee black, right?"

"That would be great, thanks," Garrett said.

"I'll give Caroline a call."

She walked away and Garrett stood there for a second, drowning in vulnerability as he tried to figure out what to say to his son. Garrett feared that no amount of self-humbling would ever open Steven's heart to forgive him.

"May I?" Garrett motioned to a chair.

"Whatever." Sketch tapped on his keyboard, not looking up.

Garrett shifted into the chair and leaned forward. He needed to say it, even if his son wouldn't listen. "I really screwed up, buddy. But don't punish your grandmother because of my mistakes. She loves you so much. You don't realize how lucky you are."

His fingers froze on the keyboard and he glared at Garrett. "Yeah, I'm so lucky I'm the town whipping boy, my father abandons me and my mother dumps me because she—" he made quotes with his fingers "—doesn't know what to do with me anymore."

"Your mom loves you, and your dad is doing the best he can."

"He's not my dad. You're not my dad. My dad's dead, just like Mom said when I was a little kid."

Silence stretched between them as Sketch refocused on his computer.

"Telling you your dad was dead, well, that wasn't my idea."

"The first lie," he muttered. "I should have known there were more to come."

"How did you find out about me being alive?"

"I couldn't find a record of your death so I challenged Mom and she finally admitted the truth."

"And that's when you started getting into arguments with your stepfather?"

"I guess."

"Do me a favor and think for a second about how hard he tried to be a good father but he always feared he'd fall short because he wasn't your biological dad. It takes a brave guy to raise someone else's son."

"He's not brave, he's a dictator. He criticizes everything I do. I hate him."

"Comes with the job description."

"Huh?"

Sketch looked up at Garrett, who fought the flood of emotions gripping his chest. "I read somewhere that teenagers are supposed to hate their parents."

"Yeah, where, in some psychology textbook?"

"Look, Sketch, go ahead and hate me, despise me, take a swing at me if you want to. I probably deserve it. But don't shut me out. I've just found you and—"

"Why didn't you come sooner?" Steven croaked.

That sound, the crack in his voice, squeezed the knot tighter in Garrett's chest.

"Look, I sent you and your mom away years ago to protect you from a killer who was after me," Garrett said. "But I was there, every year on your birthday. The pizza parties, the water park. I was close by, watching."

"What am I supposed to say to that?" Sketch stared blankly at his computer screen.

"That you'll give me a chance?"

Sketch didn't answer and Garrett didn't want to

push. He'd found his son. That's what mattered most. Sketch was safe and unharmed.

"I thought you were kinda cool at the hospital, the way you talked to me and asked for my help." He snapped his attention to Garrett. "Unless that was some kind of game to get on my good side."

"I don't play games, especially not with the people I care about. But I'm not the only one who cares, Sketch. There are half a dozen people trying to calm down your grandmother. Did you really think it was a good idea to leave the people who love you back in Port Whisper and go out on your own at seventeen?"

Sketch shrugged.

Lana approached the table and handed Sketch his drink. "Ashley's brokenhearted."

"She's better off."

"Don't say that," Garrett challenged.

"You have no right to tell me what to do," Sketch countered.

Garrett shut off the computer and Sketch glared at him. Good, at least he still had his fighting spirit.

"Stop feeling sorry for yourself," Garrett said. "I happen to know you're bright and creative and I hear you take care of the people you love. That's incredibly mature behavior for a seventeen-year-old. Do not let my inferior parenting hold you back, got it?"

"We all make mistakes," Lana offered, sitting next to Garrett.

He was glad she'd returned, bringing her positive outlook and gentle nature to the table.

Garrett's phone vibrated and he ignored it, staying focused on his son.

"Isn't that your phone?" Sketch said.

"We aren't finished."

"I am. For a guy who considers himself a bad parent, you just said all the right things. Don't blow it with a lecture."

Garrett wasn't sure how to respond to that one.

Then Sketch cracked a wry smile.

"Are you busting my chops?" Garrett glanced at Lana. "He's busting my chops, isn't he?"

"That would be my guess." She smiled.

And in that moment, a warmth crept over Garrett he'd never felt before, warmth and an intimate sense of connection with the two people sitting at the table.

"So, what's happening with the case?" Sketch asked.

"I can't discuss—"

"Come on, I'm not a kid," Sketch argued.

Ah, the inconsistency of a teenager's behavior, teasing one minute and arguing the next.

"The killer has taken another victim," Garrett said.

"In Port Whisper?"

"No, Olympia."

"And there have been other victims in other parts of the state?"

"Yes."

"What's the connection?" Sketch asked.

"We're not sure."

He turned on the computer. "What do they have in common?"

"Really, Steven, I can't talk about it."

"I can find out with a few tricks I've learned hacking into—"

"Stop." Garrett put up his hand. "You can't tell me about your illegal activity. I'd be obligated to do something about it."

"Who says it's illegal?" He focused on the screen. "Let's see, missing persons who turn up dead a few days later under suspicious circumstances." He tapped on the keyboard. "Here's a guy, Owen Crane of Kelso, found his body back in July." Sketch sipped his triple shot latte. "Then a month later, a similar death, Lars Gunderson."

"How could you know that?" Garrett challenged.

"Mrs. Gunderson tried using the media to find her husband, but he died anyway. They found his body a few days later." Sketch looked up at Garrett. "Then we have Rick Washburn. Give me a few minutes and I'll tell you what they all have in common."

"Steven—"

Lana stopped his protest by placing a gentle hand on his arm. Fine, he'd trust her instincts. She obviously thought Sketch needed to prove something to his father to earn his love.

The boy didn't have to do anything or prove anything. Garrett loved him the minute he had laid eyes on him seventeen years ago, and had never stopped.

Garrett's phone buzzed again.

"You'd better get that," Sketch said, not looking up from his computer screen.

Garrett ripped the phone off his belt, hit the password to unlock the screen and opened his email.

I missed you in Olympia, Agent Drake.

The killer. He knew Garrett wasn't at the drop, which meant the killer was at the mall in Olympia? The email also meant the killer was now targeting Garrett.

"What is it?" Lana asked.

"Work." He closed the email and called his IT guy, but the call went to voice mail.

"What time is it back east?" he muttered.

"Three hours later would make it about lunchtime," Sketch said.

Garrett paced to the front window and called Georgia.

"Agent Hunt."

"I got an email from the killer." Garrett scanned the street, suddenly paranoid.

"He's never contacted any of us directly before."

"He said he missed me in Olympia."

"He was there?"

"Sounds like it. I need someone to trace the email."

"Call Sackett."

"It went into voice mail."

"I'll try and find somebody else."

"Thanks."

Just as Garrett ended the call, Sketch reached around and snatched the phone out of his hand.

"Steven, give me—"

"You need a trace? I'll do it."

"No, we have staff who can do this."

"Who are obviously on a long lunch break." He shook his head.

"Give me the phone."

Instead, Sketch sat at his computer and hooked something up to Garrett's phone.

"Sketch, no." Garrett unhooked it.

"Then give me your sign-in information."

"You know I can't do that."

"Don't freak out, you can change the password after I access your account and it will be secure again."

Garrett hesitated, but knew if he waited too long the killer could potentially erase the email once he knew Garrett had read it. He gave Sketch the sign-in information. Sketch paused when he typed in his own initials and date of birth.

"Man, didn't anyone ever tell you that your kid's birthday is the absolute worst password? You're lucky I'm forcing you to reset it."

Garrett pulled a chair closer to his son, and Lana scooted over on the other side to look at the screen. "So, what are you doing, exactly?"

"Tracing the origin of the email. Give me a few minutes. You two talk amongst yourselves." He smiled. "I have a feeling you won't mind."

Garrett glanced at Lana over his son's keyboard.

"Yep, he's always like this," she said.

"A few more seconds…" Sketch rubbed his hands

together and leaned back in his chair. "It's searching for the origin point. Almost got it…" Sketch slowly leaned forward in his chair, his proud smile fading. "Uh-oh."

"What is it?" Garrett questioned.

His son pinned him with dark eyes. "The email was sent from this coffee shop's IP address."

EIGHT

Garrett clicked into agent mode. Scanning the shop, he spotted two desktop computers in the far corner. One was being used by a teenager, and in front of another computer was a white male, forties, who fit the profile. No way, it couldn't be this easy.

"You two, go wait in the car," Garrett said.

"I'm not going anywhere," Sketch argued.

"Look, I need you to protect Lana, can you do that for me?"

"Yes, sir. But I'm still not leaving you alone."

"I'll call 9-1-1," Lana said, pulling out her phone.

Just then the suspect stood, grabbed his coffee and headed out the back door. It could be the killer, or it could be an innocent local. There was only one way to find out.

"Wait here. That's an order." Garrett followed the man and found him hesitating by a pickup truck.

"Excuse me, sir?" Garrett called.

The man turned around.

"I'm FBI Special Agent Garrett Drake." He flashed his badge. "Would you mind answering a few questions?"

"Sure."

"What's your name?"

"Scott Rushton."

"Mr. Rushton, what were you doing on the computer in there?"

"Playing solitaire online. My wife won't let me play at home. She thinks I have a problem." Scott shoved his hands into his pockets and glanced at the ground.

Was he messing with Garrett? If he kept avoiding eye contact, Garrett was going to think so.

"Where do you work?" Garrett asked.

"I install cable for Comcast."

"Are you originally from this area?"

"No, sir. I'm from Battle Ground, Washington."

About fifteen miles from where the first victim was found. A coincidence?

"What brings you to Port Ludington today?" Garrett studied his affect as he answered.

"My job. I'm on break."

"You're awfully calm for being questioned by the FBI," Garrett baited him.

"I served two tours in Iraq. I guess not much rattles me, although I'm curious why you targeted me for this interrogation."

"Does this feel like an interrogation?"

"Yes, sir, it does."

Sirens blared as two squad cars peeled into the parking lot, lights flashing. Garrett displayed his badge, while Scott raised his hands. Lana didn't waste any time calling for backup, but Garrett was pretty sure this guy wasn't the killer.

The police officers approached Garrett. He introduced himself to Officers Claussen and Mansfield.

"I was questioning this man about a case I'm currently working on." Garrett glanced at Scott. "You can put your arms down, but I'd like to see your driver's license."

Rushton pulled out his wallet and handed it to Garrett.

"Take a seat in one of the squad cars."

He did as ordered, calm and unconcerned. Then again, psychopaths were gifted at hiding thoughts, emotions, reactions of any kinds.

Garrett called the computer tech again. This time he answered.

"Sackett."

"I need a background check ASAP." Garrett read off Mr. Rushton's information and paced to the back door of the restaurant. He couldn't see Lana and Sketch from this vantage point, but figured they were okay. The danger, if there was any, was out back.

"Hang on," the IT tech said.

Garrett went back to the police officers. "I may need you to take the coffee shop's CPU as evidence."

"Yes, sir."

"Excuse me, Garrett?"

He glanced at the back door. Lana motioned him over.

"Everything okay?" he asked.

"Sketch found something."

"What do you mean?"

"He got onto the computer and—"

"He shouldn't be touching anything." Garrett glanced at Officer Claussen. "I'll be right back."

Garrett whipped open the door to find Sketch at the computer where Scott Rushton had been sitting.

"What are you doing?" Garrett said, clamping a hand on Sketch's shoulder.

When Sketch removed his hands from the keyboard Garrett realized he was wearing latex gloves.

"Don't freak." He shook his head, as if to say, did Garrett think he was stupid?

"You shouldn't be—"

"He's not your guy," Sketch said.

"How do you know?"

"Someone hacked into this IP address and sent you the email. It didn't originate from this machine. I tried to trace where it came from, but this dude's got tons of firewall protection. Wouldn't surprise me if he's a computer nerd."

"Steven, you really shouldn't—"

"Drake." Sackett came back on the line.

Garrett had almost forgotten he was on hold. "What did you find?"

"He's clean. Honorable discharge from the army, consistent employment, letters of recommendation. He installs cable, is married with two kids, his wife's a nurse. Oh, and he was on a cruise during the time Gunderson went missing."

"I need you trace an email. It was made to look like it came from a coffee shop in Port Ludington, Washington, but originated from another location."

"You got an IP address?"

"Sketch, give my tech guy the IP address of the shop." He handed the phone to Sketch. He didn't take it at first. "Please?"

Sketch snatched the phone and read it to Sackett. Without looking up, he passed the phone back to Garrett.

"I'll work on it," Sackett said. "Who was that?"

"A tech friend of mine. Call me when you find something."

"You got it."

Garrett turned to his son. "You were right about Rushton. He's not our guy. My tech analyst is going to dig deeper into the source of the email."

"He won't find anything. So, what's next, friend?" He winked.

"We get you home safe and you stay out of this case."

Sketch's smile faded. "You're welcome." He ripped off the latex gloves and marched to the front door.

"Hey, Sketch."

"I'll talk to him," Lana said. "Go ahead and finish up with the officers out back."

Garrett watched his son pace the sidewalk in front of the shop. "Make sure we don't lose him again."

"I have a feeling that's up to you."

He was about to say something, but she stopped him.

"Let's deal with that stuff later. We'll meet you by the car."

She shouldered her backpack, shot him a smile and breezed out the front door. As she said something to Sketch, he stopped pacing. Then she touched his arm and his shoulders slumped. She was giving him a pep talk. Garrett hoped she'd put in a good word for him because right now he felt like he was constantly screwing up with his kid.

The back door to the restaurant creaked open. "Agent Drake?"

Officer Claussen stood in the doorway.

"Right, sorry." Garrett headed into the back parking lot.

An hour later, as Lana combined ingredients for chicken salad, she glanced at Garrett, who'd commandeered a table up front as his workspace. He'd decided to stick close because, as he'd put it, "Someone has to be here in case you get locked in the cooler."

He was trying to keep it light, but she sensed he suspected Lana getting locked in the cooler was not a random event. He'd called a locksmith, who was presently hard at work replacing the lock.

She liked having Garrett around, not to protect her, but primarily because she could keep an eye on him. She worried about his emotional state after his argument with Sketch, and the boy's silent treatment that followed. It was an uncomfortable ride back to Port

Whisper, Garrett trying to make conversation with his son, and Sketch completely shutting him out.

Sketch was only trying to help his dad, but when Garrett had scolded him for getting involved in the case, Sketch lumped him into the same category as his stepfather: judgmental, opinionated and bossy. A dictator. Kinda reminded her of her ex-boyfriend, Vince.

Lana knew Garrett's concern was driven by a father's fear that his son was putting himself in danger. He'd gone to great lengths to protect Sketch fourteen years ago. She figured there was nothing Garrett wouldn't do to protect the teenager.

She prayed he didn't distance himself from Sketch in the process.

Placing the chicken salad in a plastic container, she glanced around her prep table. She was ready. She'd open up on time today even though this morning she wasn't so sure. Helping Garrett find Sketch had been her top priority.

Was Julie right? Was Lana getting too involved in the FBI agent's life?

She grabbed the coffeepot and walked to Garrett's table. "Figured you'd need a warm-up."

"Thanks." He didn't look up.

She didn't take it personally since he was completely absorbed in whatever he was reading on his laptop. As she went to flip the open sign, her sister tapped on the glass door.

"Hey, you," Lana greeted. "Why aren't you at work?"

"I'm taking the morning off." She glanced at Garrett. "What is he—"

"Come into the back and I'll make you a chicken salad sandwich for lunch," Lana invited, to prevent Julie from making a snide comment to or about Garrett.

"Only if you let me pay for it," Julie said.

"Sure, but you'll still get the family discount."

"You didn't come into Caroline's when you dropped Sketch off this morning."

"Had to get in to work and prep."

"You sure that's the reason?"

Lana turned to her sister. "Why, did you guys decide otherwise?"

"I thought maybe…" She leaned across the counter. "You didn't want another lecture from yours truly about your new boyfriend."

"How old are you?" Lana joked, opening the bag of croissants to make her sister a sandwich.

"Older than you, and wiser."

Lana placed a bag of carrot sticks on the counter between them. "Says the woman who pushed away the man she was meant to marry because why, exactly? I never did figure that one out."

"We're not talking about me," Julie countered. "Besides, I'm happily married now."

"After ten years of angst."

"Aren't you feisty today."

"I'm just saying. Look, it's my life, Jules. I need to make my own decisions and yes, my own mistakes."

"Like chumming up to a man with a dangerous occupation?"

"You're married to a cop."

"That doesn't count. He's a small-town cop."

"The thing is, I'm close to Sketch and I can help bridge the gap between father and son," Lana said.

"Why is that your job?" Julie crunched a carrot stick.

"It's not a job, sis. It's a calling." She grinned.

Julie rolled her eyes. "Seriously?"

"A lot of people helped me out when I was in trouble growing up. Now it's my chance to help someone else."

Lana placed a sandwich, apple and small bag of chips into a white bag and handed it to Julie. "Enjoy."

"You haven't heard a word I've said."

"No, dear sister, I've heard every single word and I appreciate how much you worry about me. But you don't have to anymore. I'm a grown woman." Looping her arm through Julie's, Lana walked her to the front door. "If I need help, you'll be the first person I call."

"You're placating me." Julie frowned.

"Love you." Lana gave her a hug and gently guided her over the threshold. She shot her a bright smile and shut the door.

When she turned, she caught Garrett studying her.

"What?" she said.

"She worries about you."

"It comes with the big-sister job description."

"But you seem perfectly capable of taking care of yourself."

"Thank you, Agent Drake. Glad somebody noticed."

"Although I have to confess I've felt that same urge to protect you."

"You're an FBI agent. You protect the world." Lana wandered to the back counter, her tummy doing a back flip.

It's not personal. He doesn't want to protect you because he finds you attractive or anything.

He followed her into the back. "So, why do we feel this need to protect you? Are you a pushover? Was your boyfriend...abusive?"

"I don't think so, and absolutely not," she said.

"But you recently broke up."

"Yes, sir, we did." And she didn't like the direction of this conversation.

"It's none of my business, right?"

"If you must know, he was judgmental and domineering." She pulled out the plastic bowl of cut-up melon, strawberries and blueberries to premake fruit cups. "He demanded I marry him and move to Santa Rosa, California." She hesitated. "Can you believe that? Marry and move away with a man who kept trying to change me."

"Why would anyone want to?"

"I know, right? I've grown up in Port Whisper and I love it here. Why would I up and move?"

"I meant, why would anyone want to change you?"

She froze and glanced at him. He shifted away from the counter as if he suddenly realized what he'd said.

"Want some fruit?" She didn't know what else to say, so she changed the subject.

The bell rang over the door and a group of six wandered into the restaurant.

"I'd better get back to work," he said.

"I'll bring a sandwich and some fruit by in a bit."

He wandered to the table in front, looking a little distracted, like he couldn't quite process their conversation. Of course not. He'd spoken his truth, without censor or reservation. She seemed to have that kind of effect on Garrett, giving him a safe space in which to open up. And she guessed opening up was not something he did often.

"Six for lunch?" she said to the group of couples.

"Actually, there will be eight of us," a middle-aged blonde woman said.

"Let's put some tables together, then."

Suddenly Garrett was there, helping her create a larger table for the customers.

"You don't have to—"

"I want to," he said, not looking up.

Ashley breezed into the dining room from the back. "Sorry I'm late." She stopped short when she spotted Garrett. "What's *he* doing here?"

"Folks, have a seat and we'll be right with you," Lana said, handing them menus. She motioned for Garrett and Ashley to join her in the back office.

Once safely out of earshot, Lana turned to the teenager. "Whatever you were about say should be a private conversation, yes?"

She nibbled at her lower lip. "Sorry. But he's a jerk," she said as if Garrett wasn't standing there.

"Really?" Lana said. "The man who did everything in his power to find your boyfriend, twice now, is a jerk. Do tell." Lana planted her hands on her hips.

"Sketch told me how he helped you, and you bossed him around and didn't even say thank-you," she said to Garrett. "You're like the rest of them. Nobody understands Sketch."

"You do," Garrett said. "And for that, I'll be forever grateful."

Ashley didn't know how to respond to that one.

"I understand he doesn't like me right now. His feelings are totally justified," Garrett said. "I hope someday we'll be able to work it out. In the meantime, I'm focused on protecting Lana and Sketch and anyone else who might get in the way of a psychopath who doesn't care who he hurts. So, can you try and tolerate me while I do my job?"

Ashley looked at Lana, who nodded her encouragement.

"I guess," Ashley said.

"How is he?" Garrett asked.

"Angry."

"But is he talking, or is he holed up in his bedroom?"

"He's back in the command center."

Garrett sighed and closed his eyes. Ashley studied him, curious.

"You have a table of eight, my dear." Lana pointed Ashley toward the dining room. "The specials are chicken salad croissant, spinach salad with feta and strawberries, and a turkey club with avocado." She cast her off and the girl snatched an order pad from behind the counter as she passed.

"He's not hiding in his room. That's good, right?" He glanced at Lana.

"It's very good."

Once again, Lana chose to keep serving through the early dinner hour. She was hoping the FBI would open the island tomorrow so she could book some tours. She enjoyed taking people to the island, and it generated a decent income.

As she wiped down the prep table with bleach water, she remembered Garrett's sweet comment about not wanting to change her. Although they were very different, they appreciated each other's fine qualities, unlike her ex, who criticized her for not pursuing a college degree, not leaving town and not broadening her worldview. She'd seen plenty of the world on her mission trips to India and Africa, but that didn't seem to count in his book.

Vince seemed to have a very specific guidebook he followed, and wanted her to do the same. In the end, Lana knew she had to follow her heart.

"Need help?" Garrett asked.

She glanced across the now-empty restaurant. "I'm good, thanks."

And better when he was around. She caught herself and pulled back on the reins. This was not a potential suitor, even if they'd made an immediate and strong connection. His world revolved around violence, as he flew off to one part of the country or another hunting killers, while Lana's life centered around her family, friends, her faith and service to community.

The only thing she and Garrett had in common was the service part, although she hoped he'd develop a relationship with his son and perhaps mend fences with Caroline. Lana had the feeling Garrett was in desperate need of a familial connection, almost as much as he needed to open his heart to God.

And what did Lana need? A good night's sleep. All the excitement plus extended restaurant hours was wearing on her.

"You should be good to go," the locksmith said, opening and closing the cooler a few times to test the new latch. "Go on, give it a try." He motioned her to step inside the cooler.

Sure, she'd been in and out of it all day, but she was too busy to think about anything but grabbing more cheese, more fruit, or more greens, to fill the refrigerator beside her prep table.

"I'll try it," Garrett offered from the front.

He must have sensed her trepidation.

"Stay right there," she ordered. "I'm fine."

She stepped into the cooler and the door clicked shut

behind her. She took a few deep breaths, remembering how dark it was last night, how creepy. Grabbing the handle, she flung open the door, a little too excitedly, and nearly bumped into Garrett.

"What are you doing over here?" she said.

"Needed to stretch my legs."

"Sure you did." She turned to the locksmith. "What do I owe you?"

"Nothing. It was prepaid." He packed up his toolbox.

"Mother," she whispered under her breath. "Well, thanks for coming out on such short notice."

"No problem. Take care."

She gave the locksmith some leftover scones as an added thank-you and flipped the closed sign. She turned to Garrett. "Can you believe my mother?"

"Sorry?"

"I really appreciate her concern, but to pay for the repair bill without even telling me? Sometimes she treats me like I'm twelve."

"She didn't pay the repair bill. I did."

"Why?"

"I was the one who destroyed the lock to get you out so I figured the least I could do was pay for the repair."

"Oh." She didn't quite know what to say to that. It was a caring gesture, something she wasn't used to from a man.

"You're welcome? Or am I in trouble?" he said with a rare, subtle smile.

It took her breath away. "Right, sorry, thank you," she said, a bit flustered.

His phone buzzed and he glanced at the caller ID. "I need to take this."

"Sure."

As she walked into the back, the low timbre of his voice drifted across the snack shop. She couldn't hear what he was saying, but he didn't sound happy.

She hoped Sketch hadn't done anything foolish to further upset his father. Having to find your missing son twice in two days, while hunting a serial killer, was a lot of pressure for even a strong man like Garrett.

To give him privacy, she grabbed the trash and went outside to throw it in the Dumpster. The setting sun lit the island across the Sound and boats sailed effortlessly across the waves. For half a second she ached for a day off to enjoy the beautiful fall weather. But being a small business owner didn't afford many opportunities for play. She wondered when Garrett had last taken a vacation. Probably years ago, if ever.

They had more in common than she thought. They were both devoted to their jobs, although in very different careers.

She tossed the garbage bag into the Dumpster and headed back to Stone Soup. Her tummy growled and she realized she hadn't eaten much today, what with Ashley taking off early, forcing Lana to play double roles as cook and server. Maybe she'd take a walk down to the Turnstyle restaurant after she locked up. Maybe Garrett would join her.

"Stop going there," she whispered to herself.

As she approached the back of her building, a man jutted around the corner, blocking her path.

The same man who'd tried to bully his way onto her boat.

She froze. "May I help you?"

"I need to get to the island." His eyes darted down the alley.

"We've temporarily canceled the tours due to a police investigation," Lana explained.

"I've got money." He whipped out a stack of bills bound with a rubber band.

"Wow," is all Lana could say. Her first thought was that it would go far to cover the expense of the next mission trip she hoped to take. Her next thought was that if someone needed to bribe his way onto the closed island, that he had to be into something illegal.

"I'm sorry," she said. "No one's allowed on the island as long as it's considered a crime scene."

"I need to get over there!"

She didn't like bullies, nor did she appreciate the fear coiling in her chest. "Sir, please don't speak to me that way. I will be happy to take you to the island once it has reopened."

"There's no time." He pulled a gun from his pocket and pointed it at her with a trembling hand. "You'll take me now."

She automatically raised her hands. "I don't have the keys on me."

"Where are they?"

"In the restaurant."

He jerked the barrel of the gun to encourage her to open the door.

Breathe. Don't panic. Garrett will see you.

And then? They'll open fire with Lana standing in the middle?

Saying a silent prayer for guidance on how to handle this situation, she opened the door and stepped inside. Her best move was to lead him into the dining area and get out of the way while Garrett disarmed the man.

"Would you like a scone?" she said, hoping Garrett would hear her.

"What?"

"Something to eat? You look hungry."

"Isn't that your purse?" He pointed to her backpack on a chair in back.

"Yes, but I keep my keys up front beneath the counter."

"Get 'em."

She took a deep breath, stepped out of the back room and got ready to duck.

Only, Garrett was gone.

NINE

"The button matched Washburn's shirt, but no prints were found other than his," Agent Hunt said. "Techs didn't find anything else of use from the cabin."

He fought back the frustration clawing up his chest.

"He's obviously moved on," she punctuated. "Listen, Garrett, Director Franklin left a few messages wanting to talk to you."

"I'll handle it. Keep me posted."

He cut short the conversation with Georgia. He didn't want to get into another argument about him needing to rejoin the team.

Garrett dialed Franklin's number.

"Franklin."

"Sir, it's Garrett Drake."

"Agent Hunt filled me in on the case. I assume you're headed back to your team in Tacoma?"

"No, sir."

"Then I'm giving you a direct order to return immediately."

"I can't, sir."

"I don't understand. Why are you determined to stay in Port Whisper?"

"I can assist the case from here, sir."

"This is against standard protocol. And not like you, Drake."

No, it wasn't, because ever since he'd joined the bureau his job had been his priority. His focus was one-dimensional—catching the killer of the hour.

"Sir, this has become personal for me," he said.

"Because the killer targeted you in an email?"

"That and—" he hesitated "—my son lives in Port Whisper. I can't leave town until we confirm Red Hollow is no longer a threat."

"Your son? I thought you were estranged from your family."

"I was—am. It was a fluke that we ran into each other."

"I'm sorry, but I still need you back with your team."

"Then I'm putting in for an emergency family leave of absence. I have plenty of time accrued from vacations I've never taken. I'd like to use that time now, sir."

Franklin didn't respond at first. "This won't be good for your career."

"I understand, sir."

Yet for once it wasn't about his career. There was something more at stake, namely his son…and Lana.

"If you're on leave, you technically shouldn't be working this or any other case."

"I understand."

"If you uncover any leads you'll contact the team leader?"

"I will, sir."

"I'll notify your team. Goodbye."

The line went dead. Gripping the phone, Garrett shook his head and felt a twinge of remorse for probably tanking his future with the FBI. But it was the right decision, the only decision to make given the circumstances.

"Agent Drake, everything okay?" Anderson Greene said, crossing the street.

"Fine, thanks."

"Is the shop still open? I wanted to pick up a few scones if she hasn't sold out."

"Lana was just closing up. Come on in." Garrett led Anderson inside. "Lana?" he called.

Nothing.

Garrett went into the back room. It was empty, but he spotted her backpack on the office chair. This made no sense. The back door was cracked open.

He went into the alley and glanced left, then right. No Lana. Garrett scanned the dock half a block away and spotted her boat pull away.

She wouldn't have left the shop without locking up, without saying goodbye to Garrett. And where would she be going at this time of night? She was exhausted.

Squinting, he noticed a passenger sitting next to her, which meant…

He rushed into the restaurant.

"Did you find her?" Anderson said.

"Lana's in trouble. I need to get to the island." He pulled out his phone.

"Who are you calling?"

"Chief Wright."

"I passed the dock on my way here and the patrol boat was out. Scooner's your best bet. I'll call him."

Garrett paced the dining room, struggling to focus and keep his emotions in check. In this situation they were his worst enemy.

But he'd been in the restaurant all day, keeping an eye on her. How could this happen?

How did he let this happen?

"He'll meet us at his boat," Anderson said. "Want me to call Bill Roarke to lock up the snack shop? He's got keys."

"Yes, thanks," Garrett said, heading for the dock.

Anderson made the call and hobbled along behind Garrett. He shouldn't be involving civilians, but he had to get to the island and fast.

Garrett focused on Scooner's boat, remembering which one it was from the other night. He had to get there, climb aboard, and get to Lana before…

He snapped his focus to the water and caught sight of her tour boat. It was headed directly for Salish Island. If Red Hollow was her passenger, what did he want with her?

Garrett couldn't think about that now. He had to focus on making sure she was safe. He felt the sudden urge to call his son.

He whipped out his phone and called Sketch.

"Command Center."

"Sketch, it's…Dad. I wanted to make sure you were okay."

"What, I haven't seen you in fourteen years and now you're going to get all overly protective on me?"

"Sorry." He closed his eyes. "Look, can you do me a favor and stay there until I come by?"

"Can't make any promises."

"Sketch, please." Garrett heard the desperation in his own voice.

"What's wrong?"

"I can't talk about it right now. Just stay there?"

"Yeah, okay. Do you need help with something?"

"You just gave it to me, buddy. Bye."

As they approached the boat, Scooner raced up to them. "What's goin' on?"

"We need to get to Lana. Her boat's headed to Salish."

"Maybe she went out for a night cruise?" Anderson offered.

"No, someone's with her, and she wouldn't have left without telling me or locking up."

"Let's go." Scooner motioned them into his motorboat and asked Garrett to cast off. Once he did, he hopped into the boat.

"It'll take a while to catch up to her," Scooner said with a sympathetic frown.

Garrett ripped his gaze from the former navy SEAL

and fisted his hand, fighting back self-recrimination. If anything happened to her—

"Put on your flotation devices!" Scooner shouted against the whir of the motor and whoosh of wind. Anderson handed Garrett a life jacket. As he put it on he realized his lifesaver was on the boat in the distance, potentially headed to her own death.

No, it didn't fit the profile. The killer targeted aggressive, domineering males, and he wouldn't be so bold as to grab a victim in public, right in front of Garrett.

Unless this was a new element of the game: mess with Garrett's head, like he did this morning at the coffee shop by sending the email.

Which meant Red Hollow would target anyone close to Garrett as playthings. Maybe Garrett was wrong to choose family over this investigation because it put them in the line of fire. But if he'd already been targeted, no amount of backing off would change the killer's new strategy.

It was obvious to everyone where Garrett's pressure points were: his son and Lana, the new woman in his life. They'd grown close in the last few days, closer than he'd felt with anyone since…since ever. He couldn't deny it. He cared about Lana Burns, even though he shouldn't.

She filled an empty spot in his heart with her kind words and gentle encouragement. And how did he repay her kindness? By putting her in the direct path of a killer.

"Can you go faster?" he shouted to Scooner.

"Hold on!"

The second they docked Garrett jumped off the boat, tied up and went to check out Lana's tour boat. He scanned the controls, seats, floor. No blood. A good sign.

"I'm coming with you," Scooner said.

"No." Garrett glanced across the island, then back to Scooner. "You two stay back and call the chief for backup. I don't want any civilians getting hurt."

"But—"

"Please, don't argue with me on this." Garrett took off. But where should he search first? That depended on why she was brought here. Georgia said they didn't find additional evidence in the cabin, yet the killer was smart and cunning, and could have wiped everything down, bagged the evidence and sunk it in the surrounding waters of Puget Sound.

He raced toward the abandoned cabin, the most logical destination. Sprinting up the trail, his lungs labored against the steep incline. Going off trail, he plowed through a thick mass of trees, shoving branches aside.

He hoped to God he was going in the right direction, and caught himself saying a prayer.

God, I know I don't deserve to ask anything of You, but Lana's a believer. Take care of her. Help her.

"Don't! Don't do it!" Lana cried.

He broke into a sprint, ignoring the tree branches blocking his path, smacking him in the face.

Had to get to her.

Had to save her.

Had to make sure the nightmare haunting him for more than ten years didn't come true.

A flash of blue caught his eye…

Just as something slammed into his chest.

The gun flew out of his hand and he hit the ground.

"No!" Lana rushed over to him. "Garrett, open your eyes." She glared over her shoulder at the man. "Why did you do that?"

"He was going to shoot me."

"Not if you'd surrendered your weapon."

She turned back to Garrett to assess his injuries. The crazed man had swung a thick branch at Garrett's chest, leveling him.

"Garrett," she whispered. Shifting his head, she spotted a tree root poking out from the ground. She gently pressed her fingertips against his scalp and felt a lump forming. When she pulled her hand away, it was smudged with blood.

"He needs help," she said.

"Let's go."

She snapped her gaze to her abductor. "I won't leave him."

For a second she thought he was going to argue with her, maybe threaten her with the gun again. But she sensed this man was motivated by desperation, not malicious intent. Grumbling, he walked away, toward the cabin in the distance.

She whipped her cell phone out of her jeans pocket. No bars. Reception was spotty on the island, but she wasn't about to go chasing for bars while Garrett lay here, hurt and vulnerable.

"Garrett," she whispered. "You're going to be okay."

He had to be okay. Sketch just found his father. They had so much catching up to do, so many memories to create together.

And Lana had just found a man she truly admired.

"I wish I had my first aid kit from the boat," she said, stroking his hairline. "I mean, nothing in there could help your ribs, which I'm sure are going to hurt like the dickens when you wake up. But we could use a cold pack to put on that head of yours."

Pulling off her apron, she balled it up and slid it between his head and the ground, hoping the pressure would slow the bleeding.

"I'm not going to freak because I know that head wounds bleed like crazy. When I was seven I fell off my bike, right into the side mirror on Dad's car. No, I'm not kidding. Don't even try to picture that in your head. There was so much blood, I thought I was dying. And the strange thing was, once I got a look at the cut, it wasn't all that big."

The rambling helped her calm the tension threatening to make her burst into tears. Feeling helpless was the worst. She'd felt that way when she had found Dad in his worn recliner, dead from a heart attack. Lana had felt helpless when Julie had pulled away from the family after high school, and Lana routinely felt helpless when Sketch shut himself off from the world. And now he'd found his father, only to have him taken away because of some nutcase?

"I'm not letting you go, so you might as well open your eyes." She stroked hair off his forehead, leaned over and kissed him there, praying when she leaned back his eyes would blink open and he'd tell her that he was okay.

Instead, he looked even more pale. She knew head injuries could be tricky and serious.

"Look, you can't go yet. You've got an unsolved murder investigation, a son who needs you and…you haven't taken me on a date yet. I think you want to, or maybe it's that I want you to. Come on, Garrett, you need to show me how a true gentleman treats a lady. After dinner, we could take a walk along the beach. If you're here on a Sunday, I'll take you to church. You'd like our church. We're a friendly and welcoming group."

But first he had to wake up.

Out of the corner of her eye she spotted the man in the blue shirt wander toward her. He looked dazed, confused.

"What's wrong?"

Through empty eyes he said, "I have to kill you."

"Says who?"

"The man who kidnapped my brother."

"You saw him just now?" She tightened her grip around Garrett's hand.

The killer was here, on the island.

And Garrett was completely vulnerable.

"He left me a note." The man slowly raised the gun, pointing it at Lana.

She knew in his heart he didn't want to do this.

"What's your name?" she said.

"What?"

"Your name?"

"Michael."

"Like the archangel. I've been running into a lot of you Michaels lately."

"What are you talking about?"

"Michael is a warrior of God, did you know that?"

He shook his head, his eyes welling with tears.

"God would not want you to kill me, Michael. And he wouldn't want the serial killer to keep on murdering innocent people. The killer is sick. He needs help and he needs to be stopped. But shooting me won't save your brother's life."

"He's my kid brother. What am I supposed to do?" he croaked.

"Do you think your brother would want you to kill an innocent woman? To spend the rest of your life in jail because some sicko manipulated you this way?"

He didn't respond.

"Put down the gun and we'll figure it out."

"But...the note says—"

"Michael, look at this man."

Michael's gaze drifted to Garrett's still body.

"His name is Garrett. He's a warrior, too," she continued. "He hunts serial killers. He had to give up his family fourteen years ago for his job, but the most remarkable thing happened. He found his son again. Isn't it wonderful that after all those years God has brought them back together?"

"Why are you telling me this?" He slowly lowered the gun.

"Because I want you to feel hope and possibility. This man has the chance to be with his son again. You have the chance to be with your brother again, if you'd help the FBI find the killer instead of getting sucked into the killer's game. Do you think killing me will stop him? And if you kill me, what then? Are you going to kill Garrett? You can't, not after God just brought him and his son together again. Michael, please, we'll figure this out, we'll—"

"Stop talking." His shoulders sagged.

Whew, maybe she'd worn him down. A sob caught in his throat. He pointed the gun at her again. "I'm sorry."

Her heart raced as adrenaline rushed through her body. Should she try to defend herself? Lunge at him? He was ten feet away. She'd never knock the gun out of his hand before he fired.

"Please spare Garrett's life," she said. "He hasn't seen your face. He doesn't know who you are. Promise me you won't kill him."

Michael nodded.

Lana squeezed Garrett's hand and closed her eyes.

"Dear Lord, my savior, my strength. Thank You for bringing Garrett into my life, even if it was only for a short time. Please fill his heart with hope and love, and heal his wounds of remorse and guilt from which I know he'll suffer after I'm gone. Forgive Michael for what he's about to do, as I have already forgiven him. He's motivated by brotherly love. I pray that his brother will be saved and he and Michael will reunite. In the name of the Lord, Jesus Christ. Amen."

A shot rang out and she gasped.

TEN

The echo of the gunshot rang in her ears, followed by the disturbing sound of a man sobbing. Lana exhaled a quick breath. She opened her eyes and realized she hadn't been shot. Michael had fired into the air. He was on his knees, sobbing into his hands, the gun on the ground beside him.

"What…what happened?" Garrett asked in a hoarse voice.

She snapped her attention to his face, trying to focus through the tears in her eyes. "Everything's okay."

"You're crying."

She swiped at her eyes. "I do that sometimes."

He tried to sit up and winced, clutching his ribs.

"Don't, please relax," she said.

With a nod, he closed his eyes again. "What's that sound?"

"Michael is crying."

"Michael?"

"The man who forced me to bring him to the island."

"You're in danger." He tried to get up again.

"Don't, please, Garrett, you're bleeding. Wait for the paramedics."

"I'm bleeding?" He sat up and touched his head wound.

"You hit your head when you fell." She picked up her apron and pressed it against his wound. "I'm glad you're conscious."

"I heard a gunshot."

"Lana!" a man called from the bordering trees.

"Lana Burns!" a second man repeated.

"Over here!"

Scooner and Anderson burst through the trees, Scooner gripping a firearm. He quickly assessed the situation and snatched Michael's gun from the ground. Michael's eyes were pinched shut and his mouth drooped as he continued to sob.

"Police are on the way," Anderson said.

"We were going to wait but heard a gunshot," Scooner added. "What happened?"

"This is Michael," Lana introduced. "His brother has been kidnapped, he thinks by the serial killer."

"Is your brother Mark Stetsman?" Garrett asked.

He cleared his throat. "Yes."

"Why did you need to get to the island?"

"I got a call that he…was being held in the cabin. But all I found was a note telling me I had to kill her." He pointed at Lana.

"What about the other day, when you tried to force yourself onto the boat?" Garrett pressed.

"I was supposed to meet Mark to go fishing, but

didn't make it. I was late, and then the island was off-limits because of the dead body."

"We've got to get you safe," Garrett said, looking directly into Lana's eyes. Holding the apron to his head, he stood and wavered.

Lana steadied him by putting his arm around her shoulder. "Do you think you can make it back to the boat?"

"Yep. Where's my gun?"

"Here." Anderson looped a stick through the trigger guard and passed it to Garrett.

"Thanks." He pulled cuffs off his belt and tossed them to Scooner. "Cuff him."

Scooner did as ordered and they headed to the boat.

As Garrett leaned against her, she searched his face, hoping to see his eyes completely focus and the color return to his skin. His color was a little better, but he squinted, like he was still in pain.

"Lana?" he said, his focus on Scooner, Michael and Anderson up ahead.

"Yes?"

"How did you talk him out of shooting you?"

"He didn't really want to kill me. He's desperate to save his little brother."

"You didn't answer my question."

"I forgave him and asked God to forgive him. I guess he had a change of heart when he heard that."

Garrett paused, and she thought he might pass out again.

"Do you need to sit down?" She studied his eyes.

Not only were they focused, but he managed to crack a slight smile. "You are amazing, you know that?"

She shrugged. "Thanks."

Garrett continued walking with his arm around her shoulder. "I'm sorry I wasn't there to protect you."

"Don't say that. You were unconscious."

"I should have seen it coming."

"Be easy on yourself. Lots of things happen that we don't see coming."

"Yeah, no kidding."

She wondered if he could possibly be referring to their relationship.

"Are you feeling dizzy or light-headed?" she asked, loving the feel of his body leaning against hers.

"No, I'm fine."

"I'm taking you to the hospital when we dock."

He nodded.

"You didn't fight me. You must have had some sense knocked into that brain of yours."

"I have enough sense to know that the only way I'm keeping you safe is to stay close. You're on the killer's radar. Until he's caught, consider me your shadow."

She wanted him to step out of the shadows and into the light, to walk alongside her, just as they were right now. Not as an agent trailing a killer, but as a man interested in a relationship with Lana.

When she thought she was going to die, she realized what she'd regret most was leaving too soon, before she'd had a chance to explore her feelings for Garrett.

"Lana?"

She glanced at him.

"I'm not going to let anything happen to you."

With a nod, she focused on the trail ahead, sadness consuming her. He'd made a promise and she knew he'd do anything to hold true to his word, even if that meant sacrificing himself.

But she didn't want him sacrificing himself, she wanted him to open his heart to hope and love; to stop carrying around the burden of guilt she knew weighed him down from abandoning his son.

Please, God, help me show him the way.

They spent four hours at the hospital, Garrett getting X-rays and stitches. The wound wasn't serious, but he was diagnosed with a mild concussion.

He stared out the passenger window of Lana's car as they headed back to Port Whisper. She hadn't left his side all night, not when the E.R. doctor had stitched up his wound or when they'd sent him for X-rays. A good thing. He relaxed when he could see her, hear her voice. When she was close, his mind didn't run rampant with scenarios of a killer waiting for Lana after she closed up the shop or went for an evening walk.

It was past eleven and she had to be exhausted, but she didn't show it. Throughout it all, she'd stood beside Garrett with a comforting hand on his shoulder. It grounded him, kept his mind from being sucked into the vortex of guilt.

She'd almost been killed. Right in front of him.

And he'd been helpless to protect her, unconscious. Well, mostly unconscious.

Promise me you won't kill him.

He'd drifted in and out, but was pretty sure he'd heard her beg for his life. She cared about him that much. He didn't know how to process that fact. Should he remind her that intense and dangerous situations create heightened emotions? False emotions?

He was going to go with that company line? Tell her what they were feeling for each other wasn't real? How was he going to manage that when he was developing true feelings for her, as well?

"You're too quiet," she said, glancing across the front seat.

"Headache."

It wasn't a lie, but that wasn't the main thing bothering him: her life had been threatened by the killer in some kind of new game with no rules.

After all, Lana didn't fit the victimology. She wasn't a middle-aged, successful and domineering male. She was a lovely, gentle woman who didn't cave in the face of death.

"We should talk about what happens next," she said.

Like take off together to parts unknown? Because that's the only way he could truly make sure no harm came to her.

"We should both move into the Port Whisper Inn." There, he'd said it. If they lived under the same roof, she'd be close and he could protect her. And Sketch.

Yeah, like he protected her today? He massaged his temples with his fingertips.

"Stop it," she said.

"What?" He glanced at her.

"Beating yourself up about what happened today."

"How do you know that's what I'm doing?"

"A good guess?"

"Seriously, you should have been a profiler."

"So, why should we move into the inn?"

"I can keep an eye on you and there's plenty of people and activity. The killer won't risk being exposed. Caroline's setting up our rooms, and Morgan will put a twenty-four-hour watch on the house."

"When did you have time to do all that?"

"I called Morgan when you were checking in with your mom. He took care of the rest." He realized he'd done all this without consulting her. "I'm sorry that I didn't run this by you before I made the arrangements."

"It's okay. I trust your judgment."

Garrett hoped he could live up to her trust. He was questioning his own judgment since Michael Stetsman had kidnapped her and threatened her life. It was a good thing Garrett had taken a leave of absence so he could completely focus on protecting the people he cared about.

"Wait until you see Sketch's command center," she said.

"Morgan told me the kid's got surveillance set up around the perimeter of the house."

"Your kid." She winked.

He shook his head.

"What?"

"Your resilience... I mean, after everything that's happened tonight..."

"Why do I feel like you're criticizing me?"

"No, no, I'm not. I'm...impressed. I've never known anyone outside my team who can bounce back so quickly."

"What's the point of wallowing? I did that once a long time ago." She shuddered.

"After your dad died?"

"Yeah. Can we change the subject?"

"Sure, sorry."

"Don't be. It's just, well, you're right, I have been through a lot tonight and feel emotionally raw. I might look tough but the truth is, I might burst into tears if I talk about him."

"I'm sorry I brought it up." And he was. The last thing he wanted to do was add to this woman's stress level. She'd basically saved both their lives using instinct and kind words inspired by her faith.

"I'd better call in." He pulled out his cell phone and called Agent Hunt, hoping she had good news for him, like the killer had showed up on the security footage from the mall.

"You're on a leave of absence, remember?" Georgia said.

"Someone should tell Red Hollow that."

"What do you mean?"

He recounted the story, leaving out the detail about Lana begging to spare his life.

"That makes absolutely no sense, and is completely off profile. Man, this case…"

"Georgia?"

"We're no closer to finding him today than we were five months ago, and then you leave. What's the deal? I thought you were committed to the team."

"I know my leave of absence was sudden and I'm sorry. But I have to put my family first."

"Since when?"

"Since right now. I have family in Port Whisper and they might be in danger. They need me more than the team."

"I didn't even know you had family."

"Neither did I." He glanced at Lana and realized he included her in that category.

"Do you think Red Hollow is still in Port Whisper?"

"That's what my gut tells me. I'll have the local police send you the note the killer left Stetsman's brother."

"The one telling him to shoot Lana Burns?"

"Yes."

"What was the motivation behind that?"

"I'm not sure." But Garrett had his suspicions. It was the killer's way of throwing Garrett off his game. It would have messed him up big-time if she'd been murdered right in front of him.

"What aren't you telling me?" Georgia pressed.

"Give me a day to process before I theorize. I'll check in tomorrow."

"Be careful."

"Will do. Bye."

He tapped the cell phone to his knee and stared out the side window. Had Lana been threatened because he was getting too close? It was the only thing that made sense.

He suddenly wondered if moving himself and Lana into the Port Whisper Inn was a mistake. Would the better plan be to distance himself and head back to his team? No, if he did that, he'd be leaving her alone and vulnerable.

Vulnerable? This was the same woman who had talked a man out of shooting her…and Garrett.

Yet Red Hollow wouldn't be as malleable if he got his hands on her. He was a psychopath who didn't care about God or humanity. He killed for sport and Garrett wasn't going to let Lana become the next trophy mounted above his mantel.

I knew Stetsman's brother wouldn't have the guts to pull the trigger. But if he had, oh, if he had…

A woman, killed right in front of Agent Drake as he lay helpless to defend her. That would have knocked the arrogant bully down a rung or two.

What does she see in him? I can tell by her adoring eyes that she's captivated. She has fallen under his spell.

Much like my Dianna had been captivated by that brutal beast of a husband.

I shoved my hands into my trouser pockets and hovered on the property of the Port Whisper Inn. So, he's moved himself and Lana into the inn. To protect her? To bond with his son? Does everyone think they're safe because a macho cop with a gun is there to watch over them?

"Silly man." *I could stroll across the finely-cut lawn and knock on the door.*

But I'm tired. Tired of hunting, tired of killing. I exacted my revenge two bodies ago. Then I saw Washburn abusing his female companion and the ache was overpowering.

His body washing up on shore was unfortunate.

Of course, I had to kill again to divert the FBI's attention away from my sweet little town.

But Agent Drake wouldn't leave. He'd caught the scent of a fragile waif he wanted to dominate and bully. A naive girl who truly needed protecting.

The front door to the Port Whisper Inn opened and Lana wandered onto the porch, placing her hands on her cheeks. So delicate, so innocent.

Like my Dianna.

Agent Drake followed her outside and touched her shoulder, and she looked down, sad.

He hurt her. I can tell. And he would continue to hurt her unless I stop this.

"I will protect you," *I whisper.*

In Dianna's name, I will protect her.

* * *

The next morning Lana made sure she was up early so she could be around when Garrett and Caroline talked. When they'd arrived at the inn last night, Caroline had explained the alarm system and gave them each a room key. When Garrett asked about Sketch, she'd shut him down and followed up with a warning to Lana: *stay away from this man. He will only bring you heartache.*

Her words, unexpected and hurtful, drove Lana out onto the front porch. She needed fresh air, a moment to stare up at the stars and say a prayer for Caroline to release the resentment she'd been carrying all these years.

Garrett had followed her onto the porch and apologized for Caroline's behavior, but Lana told him the words were spoken from a place of incredible pain and hurt. She didn't mean to lash out at Lana that way, but she was an easy target.

After a decent night's sleep, Lana made her way downstairs to make coffee. As she filled the pot with water, she gazed outside and ached for a morning walk. But Garrett had been firm about her not leaving the house without him.

The official guests were checking out today, Sunday, and no one was booked until the next weekend. A good thing since this family needed some alone time to recover and heal.

"You beat me to it," Caroline said, wandering into the kitchen. She grabbed a gingham apron off the refrigerator door handle. "I thought you'd want to sleep in."

"I can't sleep past seven."

"About what I said last night…I'm sorry. I shouldn't have spoken so harshly. I'm so, well, I'm all over the place."

"I understand."

Caroline opened the refrigerator and pulled out a gallon of milk. "You must be exhausted after everything you've been through."

"Surprisingly enough, I'm okay. Thanks to Garrett."

Caroline's brows furrowed as she set the milk on the counter. "You know this is only a job for him."

"Yes, I know." Lana scooped fresh grounds into the coffeemaker. "You still adding a little cinnamon in your coffee?"

"Yes, I'll get it."

Caroline pulled the spice from the cabinet, measured out a teaspoon and sprinkled it over the coffee grounds in the filter.

"I think you're wrong about Garrett," Lana said.

Caroline leaned back and raised an eyebrow.

"He may have come to Port Whisper for his job, but things have changed. He's putting his family first. He took a leave of absence to protect you and Sketch."

"Probably because he's somehow put us in danger. Can't you see that after what happened last night?"

"He didn't put me in danger. A man forced me to take him to the island because a killer told him that his brother was being held captive there. Garrett came to rescue me."

"I heard you were the one who rescued him. And now he's sticking close to us because he thinks we're targets?"

"He doesn't think you're targets, but as long as there's even a remote possibility that the killer is in Port Whisper, Garrett's sticking close to his family."

"All this concern is too little, too late." Caroline pulled flour and sugar from the cupboard.

"Resentment only keeps the one holding it imprisoned, Caroline. I wish you would find it in your heart to forgive Garrett."

"Because of him I couldn't speak to my daughter or grandson for three long years!"

"That must have been horrible," Lana said calmly.

"You have no idea."

"But you can talk to Olivia now, and Sketch is living with you. I'd give anything to be able to talk to my dad."

Caroline glanced at her hand, holding a measuring cup. Lana hadn't intended to make her feel bad, but she wanted to get through to the woman.

"Don't you think it's time to move on?" Lana said. "Let God heal your anger and forgive Garrett?"

"I've been angry for so long," Caroline admitted. "I'm not sure I'd know how to live without it."

"Let it go, for your sake, for your grandson, for Garrett. He's a good man."

Caroline pursed her lips. "He's a dangerous man, Lana. He's going to hurt you. He can't help it."

"Maybe, but not intentionally. I mean, it will hurt when he leaves, but he has his life and I have mine."

"Don't make the same mistake Olivia did and think you can change him."

"Why would I want to?"

Caroline shook her head. "At least I can tell your mother I tried." She grabbed a carton of eggs. "I'm serving French toast and fruit for breakfast."

"How can I help?"

"Good morning," Garrett said, hesitating in the doorway as if waiting for permission to enter.

"Garrett," Caroline said. "Hope you slept well."

"I did, thanks."

Caroline went back to organizing ingredients for French toast. "I can whip up some breakfast for us now. Guests will be served in an hour, then they'll check out by ten."

Garrett pulled out his wallet. "Do you take credit cards?"

Caroline turned. "Excuse me?"

"For the rooms?"

"Don't be ridiculous. You're family." She went back to mixing milk and eggs for French toast.

He glanced at Lana and she smiled.

"Speaking of family, anyone seen my son this morning?"

"He's downstairs," Caroline said. "I wouldn't expect him to be conscious this early. Teenagers aren't functional until eleven."

"Downstairs is?"

"Here," Lana said, leading him to the basement door. "Unless, Caroline, do you need me to cut up fruit?"

"No, go with Garrett. I have a feeling you're a good neutralizer."

Lana opened the door to the basement and breathed a sigh of thanks. It seemed like Caroline was at least trying to be pleasant to Garrett.

"Why does he live in the basement?" Garrett asked, heading down the stairs behind her.

"He likes it down here. It's isolated and private. He can do his thing without being interrupted."

They stepped onto the cement floor and she motioned toward the command center. Three large screens filled the wall, and a cordless keyboard lay on a swivel chair. She glanced to her left and spotted Sketch, curled up, asleep on the sofa. A muted TV glowed a few feet away. It was tuned into the news channel.

"He looks so…young," Garrett whispered, wandering over to him.

"Don't tell him that. He hates it when people treat him like a kid."

Garrett winced as he sat on the coffee table. The ribs must be bothering him. But his grimace faded as he studied his son, fascinated with the sight of a sleeping teenager. It made sense since most of the time when Sketch was awake he was arguing with his father.

When Garrett reached out to touch his son's hair, Lana's breath caught. Such a tender movement from a hardened man, hardened by his job, by loss and, she suspected, hardened by the absence of faith. Garrett placed his hand ever so gently on the teenager's head, and Lana glanced away, feeling like a voyeur peering into a private moment.

A few seconds later Garrett stood, shoulders straight, and wandered to the command center.

"What does he do down here?" he whispered.

"All kinds of stuff. Writes programs, plays video games, talks to his friends online."

"I thought he didn't have any friends."

"He's got cyber friends."

"That's dangerous," he said. "They could be pedophiles."

"I'm not stupid," Sketch said in a groggy voice.

If he was awake, that meant he'd felt his father's touch a moment ago…and relished it.

Sketch sat up and groaned. "What time is it?"

"A little after seven," Garrett said.

"What's the crisis?" He yawned and stretched his arms over his head.

"No crisis. Sorry to have awakened you." Garrett started for the stairs.

"Wait," Sketch croaked, then cleared his throat. "I'm up. We might as well work."

"Work on what?" Garrett asked.

"The case." He grabbed a gray sweatshirt and flung his messenger bag over his shoulder. "Let's go."

As he bolted up the stairs, Garrett glanced at Lana for an explanation. She shrugged and they followed the teenager.

"Goin' out," Sketch announced to his grandmother.

"Where are you going?"

"Installing cameras at Lana's shop."

"Not without breakfast." She eyed Garrett. "I suppose this is your idea."

He put his hands up in self-defense. "It's the first I've heard of it."

"I don't want Sketch involved in anything dangerous."

Sketch grabbed a handful of grapes. "I'm installing security cameras at a restaurant and I'm bringing my Fed dad with me. I'm sure he's packing. How dangerous can it be?"

"Well, regardless, French toast will be ready in two minutes and you're eating before you go," Caroline said.

Sketch could have fought it, but Lana sensed he liked the fact she cared enough to make him eat breakfast, and scold his father for involving him—which he hadn't—in the murder case.

Lana helped set plates and silverware, and a few minutes later they were seated around the kitchen table enjoying the first meal of the day.

They actually got through it without any arguments. Sketch was focused on stuffing himself with syrup-soaked French toast, and Garrett seemed to be lost in his own thoughts.

"Awesome, Gran, thanks." Sketch got up and rinsed his plate.

"Delicious, Caroline, thank you," Garrett said.

"Yes, thank you," Lana added.

"Your mother expects a call this morning," Caroline said to Lana.

"Will do. We'll get Sketch back in time for church. We can all go together." She glanced at Garrett, who was already headed for the front door.

Sketch and Lana helped clear the table and went outside where they found Garrett on a phone call. He spotted them and pocketed his phone.

"Everything okay?" she asked.

"Depends on who you ask."

"Who was on the phone?" Lana unlocked the car doors.

"My ex-wife. Not very happy with me right now."

"She's never happy with me." Sketch got into the backseat and shut the door.

"Nor is my son happy with me," he muttered.

"Not true. He's just learning how to be around you. Give it time," Lana encouraged.

Lana drove to the snack shop, glancing at Sketch in the rearview. "So, hidden cameras huh?"

"Yeah, sorry I didn't do it sooner."

"Nothing to be sorry about," Lana said. Like father,

like son, both taking on responsibilities that weren't their own.

"What time do you open on Sundays?" Garrett asked.

"Not until one."

She turned the corner and spotted two squad cars in front of the shop.

"That can't be good," Sketch said. "Wait a sec, wasn't Ashley prepping this morning?"

Lana white-knuckled the steering wheel as she pulled into a parking spot. "Yes, she was."

ELEVEN

The moment the car stopped, Sketch jumped out.

"Sketch, wait," Garrett ordered.

But he was gone. Lana and Garrett took off after him.

Morgan stopped Sketch at the doorway. "Hold on, buddy. You can't go in there."

"Where's Ashley? She's in there, isn't she? Let me see her!"

"Sketch, calm down," Morgan said.

Sketch turned to Garrett and grabbed his suit jacket with trembling fingers. "It's my fault. I shouldn't have let her go to work without me, I should have—"

"You need to calm down." Gripping his son's shoulder, Garrett nodded at Chief Wright. "What's going on?"

"We got a call that the front door was busted open."

"Have you gone inside?"

"It's empty. That's what I've been trying to tell you, Sketch. Ashley's not in there."

"But…but she said she had to go in and prep early

so she could get to church." With tears in his eyes, he looked up at Garrett. "He got her, didn't he?"

The pain in his son's eyes made Garrett look away, into the shop. "We don't know that. Call her cell. Chief, I'd like to look around."

"I'm coming, too," Sketch croaked.

"Okay, but don't touch anything," Garrett said.

Lana beat them to it and marched into her shop, chin up, acting as if she wasn't scared. The chief was right beside her with Garrett and Sketch close behind.

The main dining area looked normal, chairs flipped onto tables, flower vases lined up along the mantel.

Lana went into the back room. "Everything looks fine here." She poked her head out. "I don't get it."

"Is the alarm set?" Garrett asked.

"I didn't set it when I was…when I left last night," she said.

"Bill Roarke was supposed to set it last night."

"I'll give him a call." Morgan pulled out his phone.

Sketch paced the dining room, his cell phone to his ear. Hopefully his girlfriend would answer and all would be right with the world.

"Garrett?" Lana said, looking up at him with golden-green eyes. "Why would someone break into the shop?"

"Did you check the register?"

"Oh, right, I didn't get the chance to make the deposit last night." She popped it open. "Looks like someone took the twenty dollar bills and left the rest."

"How much do you think is missing?"

"A few hundred dollars. Why not take all of it?"

"No, no!" Sketch said, on his knees by the fireplace.

Lana raced up to him. "What is it, honey?"

He held up his hand and dangling from his fingers was a silver butterfly necklace. "It's Ashley's. He's got her." Tears sprang from his eyes. "Dad, you gotta do something!"

Garrett blocked out the wounded squeak of his son's voice, the devastated look in his eyes. "Chief Wright, could you check with her parents? Find out what time she left the house this morning?"

"I'll send my deputy to the house."

"What's going on?" Ashley said, hovering in the doorway.

Shocked silence filled the room. Sketch sprinted to Ashley and pulled her into a hug so tight Garrett thought he might crack her ribs.

"Hey, what's wrong?" she said, eyeing Lana over Sketch's shoulder for an explanation.

"We thought you were…gone." Sketch's muffled voice answered.

"Gone where?"

Sketch broke the hug and wiped tears from his face with the heels of his palms. "Where were you?"

"Uh…" She glanced at Lana and nibbled her lower lip. "I overslept. Sorry."

Sketch hugged her again. Garrett walked up to his son and touched his shoulder. It was an automatic response, one he didn't have to think about. "Why don't you guys sit down and relax for a minute?"

"But I have to prep."

"I'll start prepping," Lana offered.

With a nod, Ashley broke Sketch's hold and led him to a table in the front. Garrett noticed his son didn't let go of her hand, not even when they sat down. As Sketch brushed his thumb across the back of her hand, Garrett tried to remember needing someone like this, depending on someone as much as his son depended on this girl.

"Agent Drake?" Chief Wright said.

Garrett ripped his attention from his son and went to the chief.

"There's no sign of forced entry," the chief said. "It looks like someone let themselves in."

"Just like the night Lana was locked in the cooler. Can you speak with Bill Roarke and ask him to change the locks and only give a key to Lana?"

"Sure, I'll call him."

"Sketch is going to install security cameras around the shop. By the way, in case I forget to do this later—" Garrett extended his hand "—thanks for being there for my son."

They shook hands. "My pleasure. He's a smart kid. Too smart for his own good."

"I heard that," Sketch said from the corner table.

The chief motioned Garrett outside. He was hesitant to leave Lana and kept the door open so he could see her.

"Do you think the break-in is related to your serial killer case?"

"I'm not sure, but something's off. Lana is locked in the cooler, then Stetsman's brother nearly shoots her and now this. It's almost as if the killer is trying to distract us."

"Is that what your team thinks?"

"My team." He paused. "I've taken a leave of absence until we find the killer."

"Because of Sketch or Lana Burns?" Morgan raised a brow.

"Because my gut tells me a killer is still a threat to your town, and my job is to protect potential victims."

"My job is to protect the people of Port Whisper, so we need to work together on this."

Garrett glanced up the street, and shoved his hands into his trouser pockets. "I feel like he's doing this smoke-and-mirrors act to keep us from looking at what's right in front of us."

Lana stepped out of sight. Garrett shifted a few inches and spotted her tying a blue apron around her waist.

"And what do you think is right in front of us?" Morgan asked.

"That he's local and he's thumbing his nose at us."

"Why do you think he's local?"

"Going after Lana breaks his pattern. Why do it? Because it messes with my focus and throws us off. Yet he didn't directly attack her. Why not? Because she's not the archetype he's hunting. Mark Stetsman disappeared after a book signing for *Being the Alpha Male Your Woman Needs*. The other victims had similar personality types."

"How do you suggest we proceed?"

"Our guy is most likely between the ages of thirty and fifty. Work with your deputies on a list of men within this age range who are awkward, somewhat withdrawn. The guy we're looking for was probably picked on as a kid. Although he seems self-composed, he is prone to outbursts of rage. Start there and we'll meet up tomorrow morning."

"And if we don't find him? You planning on staying at the Port Whisper Inn indefinitely?"

Garrett watched Lana pour Sketch and Ashley coffee. "I'll stay as long as it takes."

Lana wasn't sure what made her more uncomfortable at church: everyone staring at her, or the tension lines creasing Garrett's forehead. Did he think the killer would show up here, in the house of God? Well, if he did, maybe God's grace would convince him to turn himself in.

After the service she went into the community room to visit with friends. When she glanced over her shoulder to ask if Garrett wanted a cup of coffee, he was intensely focused on scanning the room for danger.

Wendy Markham approached Lana. "I heard a man tried to shoot you on the island yesterday with a machine gun."

"It wasn't a machine gun and he didn't want to shoot me."

Garrett squeezed her shoulder and she glanced at him.

"Oh, sorry, this is Garrett. Garrett, this is Wendy Markham," Lana introduced.

"The FBI agent, right?"

"Yes, ma'am."

"And Sketch's father?"

"And Sketch's father."

"It's so good to have you at church, Garrett." She leaned closer. "And so good that you've come to give Sketch some guidance. He'd better watch out or he'll end up a permanent resident of Horizon Farms."

"There's Julie," Lana interrupted. "Talk to you later, Wendy."

She grabbed Garrett's hand and practically dragged him away from the woman.

"What's Horizon Farms?" Garrett said.

"A school outside of town for troubled teenagers."

"And you pulled me away from Wendy because…?"

"I wasn't sure what was going to come out of her mouth."

Garrett stopped walking and cocked his head to study Lana. "Meaning what?"

"I'm tired of people sharing opinions about things they don't understand. Your son is a talented, compassionate and wonderful young man, but somehow he's been branded a troublemaker by people who don't even know him. It's not fair, I mean, Wendy has barely spoken to Sketch yet she's decided he's going to end up a delinquent? In my opinion if he ends up in trouble, which he won't now that you're here, it's because of people like that who make up their minds about things without having any firsthand knowledge of what they're talking about."

With a smile, Garrett squeezed her hand. "Hey, it's okay."

"You're laughing at me."

"No, I'm smiling because I appreciate how much you care about my son. You, Morgan, Caroline, you all filled in where I was absent. I can never properly thank you for that."

He gave her hand another gentle squeeze and her breath caught in her throat. His touch, warm and grounding, had a profound effect on her, and she couldn't seem to let go.

His grateful expression faded and regret took its place.

"I'm sorry, I shouldn't…" He glanced down and let go of her hand, but she wouldn't release him.

"You shouldn't what?"

He pinned her with intense brown eyes. "Caroline is right. It's dangerous to be around me."

"You heard that conversation?"

"Some of it."

"Then you also heard me say I wouldn't want to change you."

"Why not? I'm a workaholic who chases serial killers around the country. That is no way to live."

"Then why do you?"

"My job is everything. I have nothing else."

"That was before."

Eyes locked, she searched for answers, for the real reason he sacrificed himself to protect people from becoming victims of vicious crimes.

Sketch bounded up to them with Ashley by his side. "So when are we gonna blow this pop stand? I've got some ideas for…"

He eyed his father, then glanced at Lana.

"Uh-oh. I know that look."

Lana ripped her gaze from Garrett's. "What look?"

He nodded at his father. "That's the 'I don't want to talk about it and you're forcing me to talk about it' look."

Garrett pulled away from Lana. He ripped his phone off his belt and glanced at the screen.

And went white.

"Garrett?" Lana said.

He snapped his attention to the roomful of people.

"He's here."

TWELVE

"Who he?" Sketch said. "You mean the—"

Garrett placed his hand on his son's shoulder. "Keep your voice down."

"Did he send you an email?" Lana asked in a calm voice.

"Yes."

Any other woman would be panicked or hysterical. Lana planted her hands on her hips in a defensive stance. It was almost as if she believed so wholeheartedly in Garrett's ability to protect her that she wasn't scared. Well, that or maybe because she relied so heavily on her faith and they were at church.

"What did it say?" Sketch asked in a hushed whisper.

Garrett flashed the screen low to Sketch, Lana and Ashley. The message seared into his brain.

Did you enjoy the service? Too bad God will never forgive you for your sins.

"What a jerk," Sketch said.

"I'm scared," Ashley whispered.

Sketch wrapped his arm around her shoulder and pulled her close. "Don't be. My dad's here." Sketch glanced at Garrett, and the confidence Garrett read in his son's eyes felt empowering.

"Lana, I need to speak with Morgan," Garrett said.

"I'll find him." As she turned, he grabbed her hand.

"Do not leave this church, got it?"

"Yes, sir." She smiled and went in search of the chief.

"Why are we staying here if the killer is here?" Ashley said.

He eyed the girl who'd been such an important part of his son's life and wanted to assuage her fears. "The safest place is to be surrounded by people. He won't make a move in public and risk exposing his identity. Sketch, do you know how many exits the church has?"

"Two on either side, and one in the back."

Garrett glanced at the side exits. "Too bad we don't have surveillance set up in here."

Lana reappeared with Julie and Morgan.

"What's going on?" Julie asked.

Garrett plastered a fake smile on his face. It struck him that their small gathering was drawing attention.

"So good to see you again, Julie." Garrett gave her a hug and whispered, "We need to act as normal as possible. The killer may be here, in church."

"Hey, hands off my new bride," Morgan joked. Julie whispered in his ear and his smile faded. "How do you want to handle this?" he asked Garrett.

"I say slug him," Scooner Locke said as he joined the group.

"Now what kind of example would that make for young men like Sketch?" Lana offered.

"What'd I miss?" Anderson asked, approaching them.

"The Fed made a move on the chief's wife," Scooner explained.

"Bad form, Agent Drake, especially when her delightful and available sister is standing right here."

"Why, thank you, Anderson, but I'm taking some time off of romantic entanglements," Lana stated.

"You should have let me straighten Vince out for ya," Scooner said. "Pompous jerk."

"We had different life goals."

"Well, then, Agent Drake's off the list," Anderson teased.

"That's a little harsh," Scooner said.

"I'm just saying, look at how different their lives are," Anderson continued.

"Wasn't the sermon inspirational today?" Lana offered.

As they stood there, mired in small talk, Garrett strategized what to do next. First he had to get names of every male between thirty and fifty who attended church today, check it against the list the chief and his deputies were working on, then compare it to the profile.

"Garrett?" Lana's sweet voice broke his concentration.

He glanced at the group as they waited expectantly for him to answer. "Excuse me?"

"See what I mean?" Anderson joked. "His brain is so absorbed in his work that he can't pay attention to the people standing right in front of him."

"I'm sorry," Garrett apologized. "Folks, if you'll excuse me for a second, I need to have a word with the chief."

Garrett led the chief to a secluded corner of the room. "We need to cover the exits. Make a list of males between the ages of thirty and fifty who attended service today and go from there."

"How do you know he's here?"

"Sent me an email asking how I enjoyed today's service."

Morgan ran his hand across his face in frustration. "I'll find my deputy to help."

"How fast can he get here?"

"He's already here. Ninety percent of folks leave through the main door."

"You and Julie cover that exit. I'm going to see about getting the side doors locked."

"Can't, fire code."

"Okay, Lana and I will cover those. You get the front since you know everyone in town."

"Great, from there I'll be able to scan the parking lot. I'll have my deputy check the surrounding area," Morgan said. "Where will you be after church?"

"I'm not letting Lana out of my sight. I'll be at the snack shop."

"I'll swing by later."

They returned to the group. Lana had her arm

around her sister in a comforting gesture, and Ashley was leaning against Sketch's shoulder. Scooner and Anderson had moved on to another group and more small talk.

"So, what's the plan?" Sketch asked.

Garrett nodded at Lana's neighbor, Gretchen, as she passed by. "Julie, go with Morgan. Lana, you and I will watch the side doors."

"I'll call later," Lana said to her sister, giving her a hug.

Morgan and Julie wandered toward the main exit.

"Don't you think it's a little obvious if you two stand at the side exits?" Sketch said.

"What are my choices?"

"Ashley and I can do it."

"No."

"We'll text each other from across the room. It will look like a game. You and Lana hang out where you can see us, act like you're having a romantic moment. Shouldn't be hard." Sketch took Ashley's hand and walked off.

"Sketch," Garrett called, but his son wasn't listening.

Lana's warm hand slipped into Garrett's. "So, where's the best vantage point?"

"I don't like this."

"You said he wouldn't make a move in public."

"He shouldn't." Garrett couldn't be sure of anything right now, and not because the serial killer was taunting him.

Worry twisted his gut into knots as he watched his son take part in an investigation. The warmth of Lana's hand suddenly rushed up his arm to his chest. He was a mess and she was trying to ground him, but her touch only made it harder to stay focused.

He couldn't lose it now, couldn't let the killer get the upper hand because there was too much at stake for Garrett personally. But Sketch wasn't a target, he was a teenage kid, and Garrett suspected the killer toyed with Lana to throw Garrett off his game.

Yet Garrett feared that if pushed, the killer might do something radical.

"It's not true, you know," Lana said.

He glanced into her eyes. "What?"

"The email. God *will* forgive you. I'm sure He already has."

"Doesn't matter." He redirected his focus on Sketch, who broke into a full-blown smile as he gazed across the room at Ashley.

"It does matter, and not just to me, but to your son."

He eyed her again.

"Sketch would never want you to punish yourself for trying to protect him," she said. "That kind of burden weighs you down, so far down you can't see the light. Let it go and let God fill that void with love from your family."

"I gave up my family years ago."

"What about him?" She nodded toward Sketch. "Or this." She stood on tiptoe and kissed his cheek.

Clenching his jaw, the knot in his chest uncoiled

into a puddle of mush. He squeezed her hand, absorbing the warmth of her breath against his skin.

This couldn't be happening. He was a federal agent chained to his job, a man who lived and breathed violent crimes, and Lana was a small-town Christian woman who believed in the wonder of God and the comfort of community.

He released her hand, but could hardly speak past the ball in his throat. "Lana, I can't."

Not now, not when so much was at risk, especially her life.

"Sure, sorry." She blushed bright red. "I'm going to go get a cup of coffee, or a scone or muffin top. You want something?"

He wanted her, in his life, forever. "No, I—"

"I'll be right back." She shot him an embarrassed yet adorable smile and breezed off to the refreshment table.

It hit him like a baseball bat to the gut. Somehow, in the last four days, he was falling in love with this woman. So much so, he couldn't bear the thought of losing her.

Fisting his hand, he fought back the unwelcome emotion, knowing he couldn't possibly defend Lana from a killer if he was distracted. Distracted by an irrational and intense emotion he never expected to feel again.

At first he thought the adrenaline seesaw had thrown him off, opening his heart to her. But he couldn't keep lying to himself. Somehow he was falling in love with Lana.

If he truly cared about her, he'd get his act together, shelve the emotions and keep her at a distance until the case was over and she was out of danger. Because deep in the core of his very soul, he feared Caroline's words were true, that he was a dangerous man who would only bring Lana heartache.

She never should have kissed him, she thought as she tossed the salad special later that afternoon. She wasn't usually so forward. But at that moment when she encouraged him to embrace God's forgiveness and fill the void of guilt with love from his family, she was stunned by the look in his eyes: the look of complete and utter devastation. She couldn't stand the pain she read there and found herself acting without thinking, trying to do something to let him know he was loved.

Love. Boy, did she fall into a hole this time around. She'd developed feelings for a man whose life revolved around violence, a man who traveled like a nomad from city to city, chasing the evil that hid in shadows and threatened innocent people. It was an honorable career, sure, but she wondered if he chose to stay with it so long to ease the guilt of not catching the killer soon enough to save his marriage, his family.

He'd obviously never forgiven himself.

The afternoon whizzed by as she prepared food and served customers while her self-appointed bodyguard sat at the corner table. Garrett had barely spoken to her after the kiss, except to ask for more water. Apparently, he'd left his trusty water bottle in his room at the inn. Was the kiss too distracting? Or maybe it was simply that he didn't like it. Yet in that moment, the way he had whispered her name, breathed against her skin…

"Are we closing soon?" Ashley asked as she approached the counter with a tray of dirty dishes.

Lana ripped her gaze from Garrett. It was nearly six-thirty. "Yep, after the customer picks up this salad, we're done."

"Awesome. I wanted to bring Sketch some dessert to cheer him up."

Ashley dumped some dishes in the soaking sink.

"He looked like he was in a pretty good mood at church this morning," Lana said. "Why does he need cheering up?"

"His father is a major control freak."

"How do you figure?"

"He won't let him help with the case, ya know, like do any digging online or anything. Morgan let him help when Julie was in trouble."

"Garrett wants to protect him. I get it."

"Well, we don't."

"Okay, missy." Lana secured the salad in the container and turned to Ashley. "What would Sketch say if you decided to attend a party with Pete Lonergan and his buddies to try and get information about what they did with Sketch's laptop?"

"He'd completely freak out."

"Why?"

"Because he wouldn't want me to get hurt." She narrowed her eyes. "Totally not the same thing."

"Totally not so different. Why don't you flip the closed sign and finish clearing off tables?"

"Sure thing." Ashley breezed off.

Lana wiped down the counters, packed up leftovers to bring to the inn and tied up the garbage bag. Garrett jumped in to help when she and Ashley began to flip chairs to sweep.

But he still wasn't saying much. He didn't seem angry. He seemed uncomfortable, like he wanted to say something but didn't know how to find the right words.

Which meant he didn't share her feelings. He didn't care about her like she cared about him. She could handle that, she really could. But she couldn't handle the silence.

Half an hour later she locked up, set the alarm and they headed back to the inn. Ashley asked for a ride, so Lana couldn't speak with Garrett about the kiss or why he'd been acting so distant. She didn't look forward to that conversation.

They pulled into the driveway and Ashley jumped out with her bag of goodies for Sketch. Garrett got out of the car.

Lana took a deep breath. "Garrett, can we talk for a sec?"

"Of course." He leaned against the car, crossing his arms over his chest.

He was protecting himself, but from what?

"I wanted to apologize for kissing you," she said. "It's obvious that I made you uncomfortable."

He glanced at the ground between them, but said nothing. An ache flooded her chest. She realized a part of her wished she'd been wrong about her theory that he didn't like the kiss, didn't like her.

"That's all, I just wanted to apologize." She turned toward the house.

"Wait," he said.

Lana didn't look at him. Hadn't she embarrassed herself enough for one day?

"I wasn't offended by the kiss. Lana, please look at me."

She slowly turned around and searched his dark brown eyes.

"You have to understand, whatever it is I'm feeling for you, well, it's inappropriate and dangerous."

"You're not a dangerous man, Garrett. I know this in my heart."

"How is that possible?" he asked with a puzzling knit of his brow. "We've known each other less than a week and yet I feel closer to you than anyone else in my life."

"I know, it's wonderful, isn't it?"

"Look." He paused. "I can't protect you unless I'm thinking clearly, and I can't think clearly if my emotions are distracting me."

She had a feeling he might go there. And she was ready for him.

"Okay, how about this. We've just admitted how

we feel, now let's box it up and put it on a shelf until you catch the killer. Then we can pull it down and it will be like we're giving each other this amazing gift."

He reached out and pulled her into a gentle hug. He smelled of aftershave and coffee, and she enjoyed the feel of his starched dress shirt against her cheek.

"And now I'm giving you mixed messages," he said. "I like this one."

"Caroline's right. I'm going to hurt you."

She leaned back and looked into his eyes. "I'll consider myself warned."

"Whoa, Pops, you have got to be breaking some kind of code of ethics or something," Sketch called from the porch. His arm was draped around Ashley's shoulder. "While you've been flirting with your new girlfriend, I've been working on the case."

Garrett motioned Lana toward the house. "I thought I asked you not to—"

Lana squeezed his arm to interrupt his reprimand. "Give him a chance."

"I'm obviously outnumbered," Garrett said.

"Yeah, pretty much." Her hand slid down and off his arm. She wanted to hold on to it, but they'd made a deal: keep an emotional distance until the case was solved and the murderer caught.

They followed Sketch and Ashley into the kitchen where Caroline was fixing dinner. "I'm serving stuffed chicken breasts and rice in about half an hour."

"Sounds delicious," Garrett said.

"Well, you're all set," Scooner said, coming into the kitchen from the front hallway.

"You fixed it?" Caroline asked, hopeful.

"Replaced the faucet and the leaky trap. Better than new." He wiped his hands on a rag and smiled at Caroline.

Lana knew Garrett considered everyone a potential suspect, but he couldn't put Scooner in that category. He'd been so good to Caroline.

"So, you'll be staying for dinner?" Caroline asked, shifting her eyes down to her apron.

Sketch watched the interaction with fascination.

"I'd love to," Scooner said. "But my daughter's coming by with the grandkids."

"You could bring them, too."

Scooner burst into a hearty laugh. "I couldn't afford to replace all the knickknacks they'd destroy when they tumbled through the inn with their high-octane energy. But thanks. Rain check?"

"Sure."

"So, Agent Drake, how's the investigation?"

"Actually, I'm no longer officially involved. I've taken a temporary leave of absence."

"I'm sorry to hear that."

"Sorry to hear what?" Anderson said, stepping up behind Scooner.

"Ah, there's my trusty assistant. Don't know what I'm going to do without you when your travel schedule picks up," Scooner said.

"So?" Anderson eyed Garrett. "What'd I miss?"

"Agent Drake took a leave of absence from the FBI," Scooner said.

"How will they catch the killer without you?" Anderson asked with a concerned frown.

"Agent Hunt is a capable team leader. Sounds like they're making progress."

"Without you? I doubt it," Sketch said.

"Anyway, my son needs to show me some project he's working on downstairs, so if you gentlemen will excuse us." With a nod, Garrett followed Sketch.

"Nothing like a little father-son bonding time," Anderson said.

"Well, we're off. Ladies." Scooner nodded.

"Thank you so much," Caroline said.

"My sincere pleasure."

The men left, and Lana and Ashley helped Caroline get dinner ready while the guys worked on the case downstairs.

Even though the threat was still out there, a sense of peace washed over Lana. Garrett had admitted his feelings and explained his need to stay focused.

She respected his professional instincts and would give him the space he needed.

After dinner, Sketch, Morgan and Lana went back downstairs to look at the research Sketch was working on.

"So I took the list of local guys that fit the profile

and dumped it into a program that identifies connections between the men and the murder victims. Nothing hit directly."

"Maybe he's working up to his real target or…" Garrett's voice trailed off.

"Or what?" Sketch pressed.

"This started with his intended target or targets, but it wasn't satisfying enough, so he's evolving. Now he kidnaps aggressive, domineering men, asks for ransom to torture both the victim and the families, and has no intention of releasing them. Then he poses them in a very specific way that has significance to the killer."

"So, did he go after Lana to distract you because you're close to figuring this out, or because you have a similar personality type to his victims?"

"Maybe a little of both," Garrett said, taking a contemplative sip of his water bottle. "What if he started asking for ransom money to establish his identity, to make us think the crimes started there, when in fact they started before that?"

"Wait, I designed a new program that might help."

As Sketch clicked on the keyboard, Lana found herself automatically stroking Garrett's back in a calming gesture. A few minutes passed, Garrett and Lana fascinated by the images opening and closing on Sketch's screen.

"Okay, so I entered your victims' names into this program and asked it to compare them to strange or violent deaths in the state of Washington in the past six months. My program made a connection between your victims and two other guys. Greg Hopper and Teddy King."

"What's the connection?"

Sketch hit Return on his keyboard and a woman's face popped up on the screen. She was fiftyish with blond hair and sad eyes. "Dianna Baker King of Vancouver, Washington. Seven months ago she died in a car accident when she drifted into oncoming traffic."

Garrett rubbed his temples and closed his eyes briefly.

"Hey, you okay?" Lana said.

"Yeah, yeah." Garrett refocused on the computer screen. "So what about this Dianna King?"

"Guys keep dying around her. Check it out." Sketch hit Return and photos of three men popped onto the screen beside Dianna's. "She dies in February, then her abusive husband, Teddy, dies in March in Vancouver, Washington, when he falls asleep with a cigarette in his hand and burns the house down. Dianna's boss, Greg Hopper, fired her in January, and in April he's found dead in Portland—only fifteen minutes from Vancouver—from a heart attack. Not suspicious, right? So there's no autopsy."

"But there are plenty of ways to make someone look like they had a heart attack. Continue."

"You said Owen Crane, also found in Vancouver, Washington, was your first official victim with the whole ransom note thing? So get this, he was part of the consulting team that downsized Dianna's company, which forced Hopper to fire her. Then your second victim, Lars Gunderson, disappeared from the ferry dock in Mukilteo in August. You ready for this? He was Dianna's high school boyfriend."

"What else have you got on Dianna King?"

"Administrative assistant at a financial company in Portland. No record, not even a speeding ticket. Whoa." He leaned forward and eyed the screen. "But her husband had his share of drunk and disorderlies. Dianna ended up in the E.R. a coupla times with bruises, but wouldn't press charges."

"How sad," Lana whispered. "And then to die in a car accident."

Sketch glanced at Garrett, and Garrett wondered if he and his son were thinking the same thing. Perhaps it wasn't an accident and she'd chosen to end her misery. This gave Garrett a thought.

"The killer's victims are domineering men, much like her husband, which could mean he's an avenging type. He's avenging Dianna's death, punishing anyone who wronged her. Any connection between Dianna and Washburn or Stetsman?"

Sketch's fingers flew over the keyboard. "No, sir."

Garrett paced the basement. "Washburn washed up on the island, which I don't think was the killer's intent. He had no problem neutralizing Owen Crane and Lars Gunderson, yet Rick Washburn somehow escapes and drowns. The only way that happens is if the killer is unable to restrain his victim due to a physical challenge. That could also be why he's hunting close to home. It's convenient."

"You think he got hurt after Gunderson's kidnapping?"

"Perhaps," Garrett said, staring at the screen. "So, Dianna King's death was the stressor, the killer starts with her husband and former boss, but doesn't leave a signature so we won't make the connection. This is good, Sketch, really good."

Sketch yawned. "Thanks."

"Hey, ya know, let's pick this up tomorrow morning," Garrett said.

"You sure?"

"Absolutely."

Sketch swung his legs off the desk and meandered to the sofa. "Let me sleep in, okay?"

"Seven-thirty?" Garrett teased.

"Now who's busting whose chops?" Sketch flopped on the sofa and crossed his arms over his chest.

"Good night," Garrett said.

"Good night, Dad."

Lana's heart leaped with hope. They'd shared a comfortable, teasing moment and it came so naturally, like they'd known each other for years.

Garrett followed her upstairs to the kitchen. The house was quiet. Caroline had called down an hour ago that she was heading to bed.

"I'm going to make sure everything's locked up," Garrett said.

"Okay, see you tomorrow." Lana smiled and wandered to the stairs. She didn't want to distract him with a kiss, even on the cheek.

She went to her room, shut the door and pressed her back against the aged wood. A week ago her life looked so different than it did tonight. She couldn't wait to see what it would look like once the case was solved.

Wandering to the window seat, she turned off the bedside lamp to enjoy the glow of the full moon. It was so peaceful outside in contrast to what was going on in town.

She said a silent prayer for everyone's safety and got up to get ready for bed. As she passed her backpack, her phone beeped with a text message. She slipped it out of the side pocket and recognized Garrett's number from the area code.

She opened the message.

Can we talk?

She typed:

Sure!
Back porch in 5

She pocketed her phone and wondered if he'd been affected by the full moon, as well. Well, either that, or he wanted to talk about the case, or his son, or...

"No sense analyzing it."

She touched up her blush and put on lip gloss. Pacing her small room, she realized she was nervous.

"No reason to be," she whispered to herself. They'd been honest with each other about their feelings and their fears. He'd also admitted that he cared about her.

She smiled and opened her door. Quietly creeping down the stairs so as not to wake Caroline, Lana headed for the back door. A dim light glowed from the kitchen. Lana reached for the back door and opened it, but Garrett wasn't on the porch.

"Garrett?" she whispered.

Scanning the backyard, her eyes caught on something in the distance sprawled across the ground.

Not something, someone.

Without thinking she bolted from the porch, raced across the property and kneeled beside Garrett's still body. His skin was pale and his cheek smudged with dirt. She pressed her fingertips to his neck to check for a pulse.

Something snapped around her throat, choking her.

"Oh, he's not dead. Not yet."

THIRTEEN

She jammed her fingers between the rope and her skin to loosen the pressure.

"But he will be if you keep fighting me."

Through teary eyes, she saw a gloved hand press the barrel of a gun against Garrett's temple.

"He couldn't handle it," a creepy voice whispered in her ear. "The pressure of the case, reuniting with his degenerate son, falling in love."

She could barely breathe against the pressure of the rope cutting into her windpipe.

"If you love him, you will not fight me." He repositioned the gun against Garrett's forehead.

She surrendered and stopped struggling.

"Very good. Now, we need to talk. I know just the place."

He released the stranglehold and she coughed, trying to get air. Positioned behind her, he made sure she couldn't see his face.

She caught her breath and tried to call out.

"Help," she gasped.

"And I thought you loved him." He pressed the gun to Garrett's temple again.

"No, please," Lana croaked.

Garrett moaned. "Lana."

"How sweet. He dreams about you. Time to go."

A bag was shoved over her head so she couldn't see, and probably to make her feel even more vulnerable and dependent on her attacker. The killer snapped her arm behind her back and she squeaked against the pain.

"I'm sorry, Lana. It's not you I want to hurt."

With a firm grip of her arm, she felt him lunge once, twice and heard Garrett grunt. The killer was a coward, kicking a semiconscious, helpless man.

Talk about helpless, Lana was being led away by a serial killer and there was nothing she could do to defend herself. But this wasn't about Lana. It was about Garrett. This maniac wanted to destroy him.

She knew the farther away the killer took her, the less likely she'd survive. They walked for another minute and he stopped, unlocked a car door with a beep and opened it.

"Watch your head."

The horn, she'd slam her fist on the horn the minute he closed the door.

He guided her into the passenger seat, her heart racing, adrenaline pumping as she started at the mass of black surrounding her.

She was about to swing in the direction of the horn when something pricked her arm.

"Ouch! What was that?"

"Something to relieve the stress. Everything will be fine, my dear."

She swung her arm to nail the horn but missed. He grabbed her by the hair and yanked her back. "No, you shouldn't be driving in your condition. Relax now, let the medication do its job."

"Let me go."

"I intend to, not to worry."

Dizziness filled her head. "What's happening…"

"Just sleep. It will all be better in the morning."

"Dad! Dad, wake up!"

Garrett struggled to open his eyes. It felt like they'd been glued shut.

A shocking splash of cold water made him gasp. His eyes popped open and he squinted against the blinding sun. The sun? He was outside?

"What are you doing out here?" Sketch asked.

"Out where?"

As Sketch helped Garrett sit up, he glanced around the backyard. The backyard?

"Where's Lana?" Garrett asked.

"Still asleep, I guess."

"Help me upstairs."

With an arm around his son's shoulder, Garrett stumbled across the yard to the porch. He climbed the steps, pain lancing through his ribs. What had happened last night?

Caroline held the door open. "Olivia never told me that you were a sleepwalker."

"I'm not."

"Then what—"

"I don't know. Sketch, upstairs."

"Good idea, you lie down and get some rest," Caroline said.

Garrett wasn't going to correct her, wasn't going to tell her that he was riddled with panic over the thought of his freakish dream being a reality: a killer had taken Lana hostage.

They climbed to the second floor and approached her room. Garrett tapped on the door with his knuckles. "Lana? Lana, you in there?" He turned to Sketch. "What time is it?"

"Eight-thirty."

"She doesn't sleep past seven." He turned the door handle and flung the door open. The room was empty and the bed was still made.

"She probably went to work," Sketch offered.

Garrett studied her room, caught sight of her backpack and opened the main compartment. He pulled out her car keys and stared at them. "She wouldn't have walked to work."

"What's going on?" Sketch asked.

"Downstairs," he said. He had to be sure, didn't want to overreact. Maybe Lana had walked to work or bummed a ride. If he kept that hope alive, he wouldn't fall to pieces.

If she was in trouble, she needed him to be coherent and sharp.

They went downstairs to the kitchen.

"Caroline, did you hear Lana leave this morning?" he asked.

She handed Garrett a cup of black coffee and he took a hearty sip.

"No, I figured she was still in her room. I've been in the kitchen since seven and she's usually up by then." She studied him. "Garrett, what's wrong?"

"I think the killer kidnapped her."

"No," Caroline whispered. "But you were here to protect us."

"He got to me, drugged me somehow. Last night I saw someone in the backyard and went to investigate, but I was disoriented and he knocked me out."

"How do we find her?" Sketch asked, calm, level-headed.

"I'll call the chief. Caroline, don't say anything to her family just yet."

"Her mother is my best friend," she protested.

"I'd rather confirm my suspicion before we upset the family. Maybe I'm overreacting, maybe she had an early meeting."

"She wouldn't have left without saying goodbye," Caroline whispered.

Her words tore at Garrett's chest.

"Sketch and I will be downstairs. Send Morgan down when he gets here, okay?"

With a concerned frown she said, "I'm sorry."

"For what?"

"That I've been angry with you for so long, that this is happening to you again. I never understood what you must have gone through until just now."

Silence blanketed the kitchen.

"Can you really find her?" she asked.

"Yes, ma'am, with help from my son, I'm confident we will find her."

But as he and Sketch headed downstairs, Garrett couldn't help but wonder if he'd find her alive. No, he couldn't think that way. He had to seriously detach from his emotions and work the case, like all the rest.

He placed the call to Morgan, then he called Georgia Hunt.

"You think her disappearance is related to the case?" she asked.

"Absolutely."

"And you were, what, last night? Disoriented?"

"Yes."

A long pause, then, "And you think you were drugged."

"What's with all the questions? A woman is missing, potentially Red Hollow's next victim." He paced the basement, growing more frustrated by the minute.

"Garrett, we have a suspect in custody."

"What?" He couldn't process what she was saying.

"Carl Phelps. We found Mark Stetsman's body in the trunk of his car."

"But that's completely—"

"Like you said, he was escalating. He got sloppy."

"And left a dead body in his car? You know that's too easy."

"Maybe he was tired and wanted to get caught."

"Georgia, this is wrong."

"Why, because you can't play hero and save your girlfriend?" She hesitated. "Look, we've got our guy, and you're on a leave of absence so I shouldn't even be talking to you about the case."

"Georgia, I need—"

"What you need is to take a break. You've been idling at high speed for so long you were bound to burn out, and now you're imagining a conspiracy where there is none. Relax, take time to get to know your son."

"A woman is missing."

"Were there signs of foul play? Did the supposed kidnapper leave a ransom note?"

"No, but—"

"She's probably out having tea with friends or whatever they do in small towns. I've gotta go."

She hung up, and Garrett stared blindly across the basement at a stack of boxes.

"You okay?" Sketch asked.

No, he really wasn't okay. He'd been cut off from his work, the very center of his existence for the past seventeen years. They no longer seemed to trust his instincts. They were treating him like a burned-out head case.

"Dad?"

Sketch's voice cut through the haze filling Garrett's thoughts. He walked up behind Sketch and glanced at the screens. "We're on our own. Do you have a program that can take the list of men from church yesterday and check that against Dianna Baker King? There's gotta be a connection."

"Sure, give me a minute."

Garrett continued his mindless pacing, wishing the killer would have come directly after him instead of kidnapping Lana. He struggled to remember what, exactly, happened last night. He was checking the back door when he spotted a man in the backyard.

Garrett opened the door and climbed the steps, but as he crossed the yard the ground seemed to shift beneath his feet. He didn't care. The guy was too close to the house. Lana, Sketch and Caroline were inside. If the stranger got past Garrett...

He stumbled toward the figure who had his back to Garrett.

The guy spun around...

And swung a baton into Garrett's stomach, nailing his already bruised ribs and knocking the wind from his lungs. Garrett went down, clutching his ribs. He glanced up to get a look at the guy, but he was wearing a bandanna around his nose and mouth, dark sunglasses and a hooded sweatshirt.

The guy hit Garrett again, three or four times, the last time in the head. His brain spun as he struggled to catch his breath. He felt the guy take Garrett's phone off his belt, saw him send a text, and toss the phone on the ground. Garrett struggled to get up, but he could barely focus.

Have some more water, Agent Drake. His attacker gripped Garrett's jaw and poured water in his mouth. Garrett tried spitting it out, but swallowed some, and that made him wonder if the killer had spiked his water bottle.

That's a good boy.

Then he heard Lana gasp for help.

And he could do nothing to protect her.

"Dad!" Sketch said.

Garrett spun around. "Sorry."

"We've got half a dozen hits because Dianna Baker King and her family lived in Port Whisper thirty years ago, so here are the guys who also lived here." He handed him a printout of six names, including Scooner Locke, Bill Roarke and Anderson Greene.

The basement door whipped open and Morgan flew down the stairs.

"What can you tell me about these men?" Garrett handed Morgan the list.

"Wait, you've gotta see something. Sketch, move."

The kid jumped out of his chair and Morgan sat down.

"What is it?" Garrett asked.

"I got an email this morning." He signed into his account and opened an email from Phelps2114@vyenet.com.

"Phelps," Garrett muttered. "My team has a guy named Phelps in custody."

"It's a link to a video feed."

Morgan clicked on the link. It opened to an image of Lana asleep on a cot in a small room. A figure approached her with his back to the camera. He held something up to the camera so they'd be sure to see it.

Red hollow braided rope.

FOURTEEN

With a moan, Lana massaged her temples with her fingertips and opened her eyes.

It took her a few seconds to focus on her surroundings, but once she did, anxiety arced across her chest. She was in a dark room about twelve feet square. A lamp glowed in the corner on an old-fashioned desk. Sitting up, she gripped the wool blanket covering the cot beneath her.

She remembered being taken last night, her kidnapper kicking Garrett for good measure, shoving her into his car, pricking her with some kind of drug that made her sleep.

And gave her this doozy of a headache.

Footsteps echoed against the ceiling. So, there was a floor above her. If Garrett was right, her captor was a local, which meant she knew him. Maybe she could talk him out of this nonsense, like she did with Michael on the island.

She had enough critical thinking brain cells left to

know that once she saw his face she was a definite liability. Which raised the question, why kidnap her?

To torture Garrett, of course.

There was a tap at the door. She lay down on the bed and faced the wall.

The door squeaked open and she held her breath.

"I know you're awake," he said in a gravelly voice as if trying to mask it. "I've been watching you."

Which meant he had a video camera in the room? Ick.

"I'm sorry you got involved, but someone had to defend you from that ogre."

"What ogre?"

"Agent Drake."

"What makes him an ogre?" she asked, staring at the cement wall.

"He's arrogant and domineering. He's a bully, like Vincent."

Okay, so he knew her well enough to know about her ex-boyfriend.

"I needed to save you from yourself, Dianna."

Was he having a full break with reality?

"I've brought you lunch. Maybe we'll take a drive later."

"That would be nice," she said.

"Oh, and by the way, your family can see you right now. The video feed is going directly to the police station. Garrett, Julie, Morgan, they can all see you. I wouldn't want to worry your mother."

"Can I ask you something?"

"Of course."

"What are you going to do to me?"

"Keep you safe."

A hand patted her shoulder and she clenched her jaw.

"That's all. Just keep you safe."

"No!" Garrett grabbed a nearby chair and threw it across the basement. Heart pounding, he couldn't think past the image of the killer touching her with one hand, while gripping the rope with the other.

He was messing with all of them.

"So help me…" was all he could get out.

He whipped out his phone and called Georgia, but it went directly to voice mail. He called the IT specialist.

"Sackett."

"It's Drake. I need—"

"Can't talk to you. Orders."

"Listen to me," Garrett protested, but the line had already gone dead.

"He hasn't killed her," Morgan said. "What do you think he wants?"

"Me."

"Then he's already won," Sketch said.

Garrett and Morgan glared at the teenager.

"What? This crazy throwing chairs stuff is his goal. You can't catch him if you're messed up beyond the point of rational thought."

Garrett eyed Morgan.

"I know, old for his years," Morgan said.

"And smart for seventeen. Okay, Red Hollow wants to get at me by driving me insane, so he'll want to drag this out. Sketch, see what you can find out about that video feed."

"Already on it."

"Morgan, look at this list of six men who fit the profile and were connected to Dianna Baker King."

"Who?"

"It's a theory we're working on. What can you tell me about these guys, especially Bill Roarke and Scooner Locke?"

"Why them?"

"They were in town about the same time Dianna Baker King lived here as a child, and were about her age. I think the killer is avenging her death. Maybe he had a childhood romance with Dianna or they were classmates or something."

As they went through the list of names, Garrett fisted and unfisted his hand to maintain what his son so deftly referred to as rational thought.

The kitchen door opened and Caroline came halfway downstairs. "What's happening?"

"We need a little more time," Garrett said.

"Scooner's coming over for biscuits, or should I tell him not to?"

Sketch glanced at Garrett.

"No, actually, we could use his help," Garrett said.

"Okay, I'll make enough biscuits for everyone, then."

"Thanks," Garrett said.

She went back into the kitchen and Garrett mo-

tioned for Sketch to close the door. He raced up there
shut it quietly and came back down.

"If Scooner's the guy, and he's got a thing for Gran..."

"Calm down. We don't know for sure that it's him,"
Garrett said.

"Want me to call my deputy?" Morgan said.

"Not yet. Let's stay calm. Go upstairs and ask him
some questions, see how he reacts."

"Hey, Dad?"

Garrett glanced at his son, working furiously on
his keyboard.

"You're thinking it's a guy who's had contact with
Dianna about thirty-five-ish years ago?"

"That makes the most sense, but maybe it's someone
who's been holding a torch for her since she moved
away."

"I doubt Bill Roarke is your guy," Sketch said,
pointing to a screen. "He's happily married with three
grown kids, five grandkids. He babysits on a regular
basis. Would be kinda hard to hide victims in a basement full of Legos. Whoa." Sketch eyed the screen.

"What?" Morgan asked.

"Facebook messages between Dianna and—" He
hesitated and glanced at Garrett. "Scooner Locke."

The doorbell rang and Sketch bolted out of his chair.
Garrett caught him with an arm around his chest.
"Hang on."

"I'm not going to let her open the door to a serial
killer."

"(A) he may not be our guy and (b), he won't hurt

your grandmother, especially not in a houseful of people. Listen to me."

Sketch struggled against him.

"Want me to…" Morgan motioned to head upstairs.

"Yeah, we'll be right up."

Morgan went upstairs and shut the door.

"Let me go," Sketch protested.

"Sketch, listen."

"I won't let him hurt her, I won't."

"Look at me." Garrett turned him around with firm hands on his shoulders. Once he looked directly into his son's panicked brown eyes he said, "We're not going to let anything happen to her. You just gave me the lecture about losing rational thought. Now it's my turn. You're no good to your gran like this, right?"

Sketch clenched his jaw.

"What we need to do is go up there and act normal, engage Scooner in conversation. That's how we'll get information from him. If he's the killer, we need to be that much smarter and not let on that we suspect him. Can you trust me on this?"

"You don't understand. She's the only one who…" His voice trailed off and he glanced down.

"Not anymore she isn't. You've got me now, and Ashley and Morgan, and we're going to get Lana back. She's probably your biggest fan. You're not alone, son."

Sketch nodded, but still didn't look at Garrett.

"You ready to do this?"

"Yes, sir."

Sketch's computer beeped. He spun around and studied the screen on the left, filled with numbers.

"What is it?" Garrett asked.

"According to the IP address, the video feed is coming from the police station."

"A computer genius," Garrett muttered. "I wonder how much Scooner knows about computers."

"Let's go ask him." Sketch started up the stairs.

"Are you going to keep your cool?"

"I will if you will."

If Scooner Locke was their guy, he was doing an excellent job of masking his guilt. But then psychopaths were nothing if not charming and clever. Garrett leaned against the counter and watched the interplay between Scooner and Caroline. He seemed to genuinely adore her, much to the chagrin of Sketch. The kid tapped his fingertips against his glass coffee mug repeatedly. He was going to lose it.

"Looks like someone's had too much coffee already," Scooner joked.

"What's that supposed to mean?" Sketch leaned forward.

"Sketch, don't be rude," Caroline said.

"He's just being protective," Garrett offered.

"Yeah, Scooner, everyone knows how you feel about Caroline," Morgan added.

Caroline blushed. "Stop it. You're embarrassing me."

The room fell silent for a few seconds. Then Scooner

leaned back in his chair. Garrett had to play this just right or he'd never find out where the guy was keeping Lana, if he even was their guy.

Scooner looked squarely at Sketch. "It's true. I do care about your gran and I respect how protective you are."

"So you won't mind if I ask you a few questions?" Sketch said.

"You know everything there is to know about me, but sure, have at it."

"Actually, I'd like to ask a few," Garrett said, afraid his son might lose it and lunge across the table at Scooner if he gave the wrong answer. "You've lived in Port Whisper your whole life?"

"Other than my years as a navy SEAL, yes, sir."

"Do you happen to remember a girl named Dianna Baker?"

Scooner glanced into his coffee. "Yes, I remember her."

"Why aren't you looking at me, Scooner?"

Morgan got up and wandered to the coffeepot, which was located conveniently by one of the kitchen exits. Garrett was blocking the other one.

"Because I feel ashamed when I hear her name," Scooner said.

"Why do you feel ashamed?"

"I don't understand, who is Dianna Baker?" Caroline said.

Garrett put up his hand to silence her.

"Scooner?" Garrett pressed.

He glared at Garrett. "Because I shoulda figured out she was asking for my help, but I didn't, and now she's dead."

"Scooner," Caroline whispered.

"She died in a car accident," Garrett said.

"Probably because she was trying to get away from that abusive husband of hers."

"How did you know about her husband?" Garrett asked.

"She found me on Facebook about a year ago."

"You knew her growing up?" Garrett continued.

"Yes, sir. We were classmates through the ninth grade until they moved away. I had the biggest crush on her, poor kid."

"Poor kid?"

"Her father was a monster. Had a thing for bourbon and smacked his kids around."

"Kids? There were more than one in that family?" Morgan asked.

"Yep, she had a little brother, what was his name…? Jack, I think. Jack Baker. Squirrely kid, with thick glasses and freckles. The kids teased him at school. The old man hit him at home. She'd get whacked trying to defend him against the dad. I wanted to help, but who was I? Some punk fourteen-year-old. I told my folks, but back then no one knew what to do about that kind of thing. Everyone figured what happens in a family stays in a family." He suddenly looked up. "Why are you asking?"

"Hang on." Garrett put his hand on his son's shoulder. "Downstairs, everything you can find on Jack Baker."

"Got it." Sketch tore off.

"You think—"

"Makes sense," Garrett interrupted Morgan.

"What are you guys talking about?" Scooner asked, glancing from Garrett to Morgan back to Garrett.

"I think the serial killer knew her growing up and is exacting revenge on the stepfather by killing men who have wronged her, or resemble her stepfather," Garrett explained.

"She told me about her abusive husband and overbearing boss. I felt so bad for her, I mean, first her father, then her husband."

"Did she mention her brother at all?"

"She said he'd been married and divorced, and moved back to this area. He must be, what, mid- to late forties?"

Garrett shared a knowing glance with Morgan. It fit.

"Did she say how long ago her brother moved back?"

"No, sir, she didn't."

Garrett's phone vibrated. He ripped it off his belt, but didn't recognize the number.

"Yes," he answered.

"Garrett?"

He gripped the phone tighter. "Lana?"

"Hey, yeah, it's me."

Garrett raced into the basement, leaned over Sketch's shoulder and studied the screen where Lana sat on the cot clutching the phone.

"Hey, sweetheart, how you holding up?" Garrett asked.

"Oh, you know me..."

"How did you get the phone?"

"He left it for me so I could call you."

"Do you recognize his voice?"

"Sort of, but he's trying to mask it. I haven't looked at him because I figured if I don't know who he is, he has no reason to kill me."

"Smart girl. Now look at the camera mounted on the wall. I can see you."

She put up her hand in a halfhearted wave. He could tell she was scared senseless, but was keeping it under control.

"We're going to figure out where you are," Garrett said.

"I know you will." As she said the words, her gaze drifted to the floor. "I'm sorry he's doing this to you, Garrett."

"You have nothing to be sorry about. I want you to focus on your surroundings. Is there a window in your room?"

"Yes, but it's small and it has bars over it. I think I'm in a lower level."

"Can you open the window?"

"I think so." She scooted a chair across the room.

Garrett couldn't take his eyes off the door, worried that the killer might return and hurt her.

"It's open," she said.

"What do you hear and smell?"

She tipped her nose. Garrett could hear her breathing.

"A sweet smell, like lilacs..."

"Sounds?"

"It's quiet." She glanced up at the ceiling. "Footsteps. Garrett, he's coming back."

"It's okay, I'm right here." His heart sped up. He leaned closer to the monitor, looking for something, anything to give him a clue as to where she was.

She buried her face in one hand and held the phone with the other. "Garrett, you have to promise me you won't blame yourself for whatever happens."

"Lana—"

"Promise," she said more firmly.

"I promise."

The door to her room opened and the killer stepped inside. "Lana, it's okay, his face is covered," Garrett said.

It was covered once again by a bandanna, sunglasses and hooded sweatshirt. He extended his hand and Lana handed him the phone.

"Sorry to cut this short, Agent Drake, but Lana and I have a date for a morning drive in the country."

"What do you want?"

"Why, I thought you would have figured that out by

now." He hesitated and looked directly at the camera lens. "I want you."

"Name the place. I'll be there."

"Really? You'd sacrifice yourself to save a woman you've known for less than a week? Now why is that?"

"She doesn't deserve to die."

"But you do, don't you? All those victims you couldn't save, abandoning your son when he was only three."

Garrett gripped the phone tighter. "You don't want a weak, submissive hostage. She's too much like Dianna, abused by powerful men her whole life."

Silence, then, "You know nothing about Dianna."

"I know you were both abused by your father, then she married an abuser. And you couldn't help her, could you? But you can help Lana."

"Oh, I am helping Lana."

He dropped the phone on the nearby desk, but left it on speaker. "Time to go." He shoved a sack over Lana's head.

"Wait!" Garrett called out. "You want me, how about a trade?"

The killer stared at the camera lens. "Oh, Agent Drake, I already have you." He twisted Lana's arm behind her back and shoved her out of the room.

"Garrett, don't forget, you promised!" she called, as she was being pulled away.

He stared at the empty room. A door slammed, then nothing.

FIFTEEN

"It's right in front of us," Garrett said. "He knew I'd abandoned you when you were three. He knows how I feel about Lana. He's part of the inner circle. Let me see the list again."

Sketch handed it to him and one name jumped out as if written in bright red ink: Anderson Greene. His comments rushed back to Garrett.

Did you figure it out?

How will they catch the killer without you?

His brain is so absorbed in his work that he can't pay attention to the people standing right in front of him.

Anderson used a cane, which meant he was injured and less able to keep Washburn under control, and he was at the inn last night helping Scooner fix the plumbing. He could have easily spiked Garrett's water bottle.

"Find me everything you can on Anderson Greene," he ordered Sketch. "Including any properties he owns."

Garrett went back upstairs to question Scooner. "How long has Anderson Greene lived in town?"

"He moved here, what—" he glanced at Caroline "—about three or four years ago?"

She nodded her confirmation.

"What does he do for a living?" Garrett asked.

"Some kind of customer service position for a computer company, you know, helping people with software problems. He travels a lot, or he was traveling a lot, but his sciatica flared up so he's been working from home."

"He's probably on medication for the pain?" Garret asked.

"Yeah, I guess," Scooner said.

"Which is what he used to drug his victims. Is he married?"

"Divorced. Doesn't talk about her. No kids."

"I think he's Dianna's brother."

"No." Scooner leaned into the table. "That can't be."

"You didn't recognize him as Jack Baker when he moved back?"

"No, sir, he didn't look anything like the skinny little blond kid and he had a different name."

"He wanted a fresh start. He must have good memories of growing up here, which is why he moved back."

"Dad, I got it!" Sketch burst into the kitchen. "He owns two properties in town, and here's the make and model of his car."

Garrett handed that information to Morgan. "Put

out an all points. We need to at least bring him in for questioning."

"Oh, there's no doubt he's your guy," Sketch said. "Anderson Greene is Jack Baker. Greene is his biological father's name. He was born John Anderson Greene, which is why they called him Jack, but his father died when he was two. When Anderson was four, his mom married Tim Baker, who adopted the kids, hence the name change: Jack Baker and Dianna Baker. They lived in Port Whisper for five years when he was seven through twelve years old, then moved to Vancouver."

"So, little Jack reinvented himself using his middle name and biological father's name."

"I still can't believe he's the killer," Caroline said.

"I can."

They all looked at Scooner.

"Now that I think about it, he's short-tempered and kind of heartless. I mean, he joked about the body that floated up on Salish Island."

"Morgan, we need to search Anderson's properties. Scooner, did he ever mention places where he liked to spend time, a nearby attraction?"

"No, sorry. Wait, little Jack used to ride his bike up to the lighthouse and sneak inside. I guess he felt safe there. Used to scare Dianna. She was afraid he'd pretend he was a superhero and jump into the Sound."

"Morgan, come with me to the lighthouse. Call a judge and send your deputies to Anderson's properties to wait for a search warrant. I doubt he's inside, but if he is, he can't leave with a missing person. Scooner, you stay here and keep an eye on Caroline?"

"Absolutely."

"Let's go." Garrett started for the front of the house.

"I'm coming," Sketch announced.

"No, Sketch, I need you to stay in the command center and watch over the room. He might bring her back. Also, I need you to find his car. The lighthouse is at best a guess."

"But—"

"I seriously need you to be my tech guy, okay? I'm not placating you by asking this favor. I cannot do this without my genius son back here at the command center."

"I'll call you when I find the car."

"Good. I need you calm and confident, for your gran's sake."

"And yours?"

"And mine." Garrett gave his son a hug, turned and raced down the front steps to Morgan's Jeep. The hug was too short, too impersonal and it could have been Garrett's last.

Nope, he couldn't go there, couldn't think about the possibility that in order to save Lana's life, he'd have to sacrifice his own.

And he would, no question. Garrett was better equipped than Lana to deal with whatever emotional or physical torture Anderson had planned.

As they pulled away from the inn, Garrett realized that although their time had been short, he'd bonded with his son instantly and deeply. He was at peace with that relationship. Sketch knew his father loved him. Now, if only he could be at peace with the Lana part of his life.

Regret tore through his chest. When they had spoken on the phone, he should have told her how much he cared about her, how he didn't think it was possible to fall in love again, and definitely not so quickly. He should have told her that he would give anything to take her out on a real date, ride the ferry into downtown Seattle, and bum around Pike Place Market. He'd actually go shopping with her. Amazing.

"We're going to get her back," Morgan said, but his voice belied his confidence.

"We will. As long as we stay focused and detached."

And Garrett would do exactly that. For Lana.

His detachment disintegrated as the day grew longer with each failed attempt to find Lana. The lighthouse was locked up tight.

They checked Anderson's house, and his second property, but no luck. It was like they'd disappeared.

When they had searched Anderson's second property, a farmhouse on the outskirts of town, they found the basement room where he'd kept Lana. As they searched it, Garrett spotted something on the floor beneath the bed: Lana's silver cross charm necklace. The chain wasn't broken and the lock still functioned.

He scooped it up in his hand and closed his fingers. She'd left this on purpose, for him. Her last act was one of selflessness. She was trying to take care of him, give him strength through God.

"I'm headed back upstairs," Morgan said. "Forensics is on the way."

"I'll be up in a minute." He focused on the cool metal in his palm and surrendered.

Please, God, help me. She's a beautiful, generous, compassionate woman who deserves a full life with children and laughter. Please, help me find her.

With a deep, cleansing breath, he opened his eyes. Glancing once more around the room, he spotted something on the floor. He kneeled and touched it with his fingertips. Sand.

He got up and took the stairs two at a time. He burst into the kitchen then analyzed the floor. More sand.

He searched for Morgan, who was on the front porch talking to one of his deputies.

"Where is the closest sandy beach around here?"

"About forty minutes west, at Deception Point," Morgan paused. "And there's a lighthouse."

Garrett's phone vibrated. "Agent Drake."

"Still an agent?" Anderson taunted. "Not a very good one considering you can't find me. What's taking you so long?"

"I'm on my way."

"Really? You've figured out I'm at Whistler Pass?"

"Of course."

"Good. Bring refreshments."

"Pizza or burgers?"

Anderson chuckled, the sound hollow and menacing. "You still have your sense of humor. I'm impressed. And, Garrett, please don't bring any of your colleagues. I'd hate to have to hurt Lana."

The line went dead.

"Well?" Morgan said.

"He said he's waiting for me at Whistler Pass."

"You don't believe him."

"I think it's another diversion to mess with my head. It's all about power and control for this guy."

"What do we do?"

"You have a suit and tie?"

"Sure, why?"

"Because with your help I'm going to be in two places at once."

Lana was tired, hungry and cold. Her kidnapper had given her a wool blanket, but it did little to warm the chill from her body. Then again, maybe she was trembling for another reason.

She'd been locked inside a small room for hours, surrounded by storage boxes, the sun casting shadows across the room as it moved from east to west. She'd figured from their long trek up about forty steps, that she was in a lighthouse, but the window was too high to see out.

At one point he'd slid a paper lunch bag inside. That had been their only interaction. If he was going to kill her, what was he waiting for?

The door cracked open. "Time for some fresh air,"

he said from the hallway. "Please exit the door outside your room on the left."

She stood and walked to the door, then stepped into the hall area, not glancing over her shoulder. She was pretty sure her captor was Anderson, and she'd spent the better part of her day in solitude trying to figure out how to get through to him.

"Dinner is waiting for you out on the gallery," he said.

"Are you sure you want to do this?"

"Feed you?"

"Kill me." She hesitated as she approached the door to the outside.

"I'm not going to kill you. Not unless Agent Drake wants me to."

Now he was talking nonsense. Garrett cared about her, maybe even loved her.

The sound of a slamming door echoed up the stairs.

"Lana!" Garrett called from below.

Relief coursed through her, and she was about to respond when Anderson shoved her outside and locked the door. She huddled against the wall and clutched the wool blanket tighter around her shoulders.

What if Anderson got the advantage and wounded Garrett? She couldn't help him if she was locked outside, fighting to stay warm against the northern wind.

A shot rang out from inside the lighthouse, followed by silence.

The door creaked open and she couldn't help but look up, hoping to see Garrett smiling down at her.

Instead, Anderson stepped out onto the gallery. "Aren't you hungry, Lana?"

"What did you do?" she shouted against the whistling wind.

"I saved you from a life of heartache and pain."

"No!"

"Anderson!" Garrett shouted from inside.

Anderson grabbed Lana's arm and yanked her to her feet. With an arm around her neck, he backed away from the door.

Footsteps reverberated against the inside walls. Lana dug her fingers into Anderson's arm, trying to free herself as Garrett stumbled outside, gripping his side with his left arm and pointing a gun with his right.

"I thought I killed you," Anderson said.

He pressed the barrel of the gun against Lana's temple and she couldn't help but close her eyes. She was going to be sick.

"Drop the gun," Anderson ordered. "You know I'll kill her."

"Why? What could you possibly have to gain by killing her?" Garrett questioned.

"Besides destroying you? Absolutely nothing."

"And why do you want to destroy me? Huh, Jack?"

"Don't call me that! Jack is a weak and pathetic little boy!" His grip tightened around Lana's neck.

"Okay." Garrett put out a hand in surrender. "Sorry."

"You are not. You're just like the rest of them. Arrogant and domineering. You'll crush this sweet woman, destroy her life. You don't care who you hurt. Look at your son, that juvenile delinquent can't even graduate high school, thanks to you."

"Let her go. You can have me." He dropped his gun and put up both hands. "I won't resist."

"No," Lana gasped. Unarmed, Garrett was an easy target.

"You'll try to overpower me," Anderson said. "She won't."

"I'm hit. How am I going to overpower you?" Garrett motioned to his bloody shirt. "Listen to me, do you really think Dianna would want you to murder innocent people in her name?"

"Innocent? Her husband brutalized her! Crane ordered her boss to cut staff and fire her. Somebody had to protect her."

"You did. You took care of them all. She's gone now. And you miss her, I get that. But something broke inside of you when she died. You need help. I can get you help."

"I need justice!" he shouted, pointing the gun at Garrett's chest.

Lana lost it and jammed her elbow into Anderson's ribs as hard as she could. He jerked forward and the gun went off, piercing her eardrums. He loosened his grip and she scrambled toward the door, as Garrett lunged over her at Anderson.

She couldn't watch, but had to, trying to figure out a way to help Garrett. Garrett gripped Anderson's firing arm, pointing the gun up at the sky. Another shot rang out and Lana bit back a scream.

Then Anderson jerked Garrett forward and kneed him in his stomach wound. Garrett fell to his knees, clutching his side.

Anderson aimed.

"No!" Lana lunged at Anderson, but he swung this arm and hit her in the side of the head with the gun. She went down, dazed…

The gun went off.

She struggled to focus through the stars filling her vision, but couldn't.

"Lana, can you hear me?"

She blinked a few times. Garrett's handsome face and caring brown eyes came into focus.

"What happened?" she said.

"You're safe." He pulled her against his chest.

Warmth spread across her shoulders as she clung to him, ignoring the harsh wind whipping through her hair.

"It's okay. It's over," he said.

Still nervous about their attacker, she cracked her eyes open and glanced over Garrett's shoulder. They were alone on the gallery.

Lana was okay, thank God. Gratitude flooded Garrett's chest, not only because she was safe, but also because he realized Lana had opened his heart to the wonder of God and community.

As she was being treated for cuts, bruises and possibly a concussion, another E.R. doc had stitched up Garrett's flesh wound. Good thing Anderson was a bad shot or this would have been a completely different ending.

Garrett lay back on the E.R. bed and closed his eyes. Lana would be fine. All was right with the world. He could breathe for the first time in a week.

"Garrett?" Lana's sweet voice said.

He opened his eyes and was struck by the odd expression on her face.

"You okay?" he said.

"Doctor says I'll be fine. A few bruises, minor concussion. You?"

"He clipped me, but it's not serious." He absently touched his side.

With a nod, her gaze drifted to the floor as if she couldn't bring herself to look at him. Of course not—the very sight of Garrett reminded her of the most violent, terrifying experience of her life. She knew the truth now, the baggage that came with knowing Garrett Drake. He was surrounded by violence and ugliness, and no matter how hard he tried, he'd never cleanse the stench of death from his skin.

Then there was Lana. A charming, delightful woman who ran a snack shop, took visitors on boat tours, looked forward to Sunday church services and spent time with her family.

They were ill suited for each other in every way that counted.

But he'd saved her life and she probably felt beholden to him. He cared about her. A lot. So he would let her go, give her permission to move on. Maybe, in time, she could put the violent images behind her.

"Can you hand me that envelope?" He pointed to the chair.

"What is it?" She passed it to him.

"A fax Georgia sent over. Three housewives have gone missing in Ohio. We've been asked to get there ASAP."

She snapped her eyes to his. "I thought you were on leave."

"Temporary."

"But—"

"They need me."

"Your son needs you."

"He'll be fine."

"Garrett—"

"I'm glad you're okay," he said, not looking up. He couldn't. It would break his heart if he lingered too long on that adorable face and those beautiful golden-green eyes.

"Really, Garrett? That's how you're going to play this?"

He glanced up. Now she was angry. Good. That fighting spirit would help her heal from the trauma of surviving a kidnapping, an attempted murder.

Of surviving Garrett in her life.

"I'm not sure what you want me to say." He winced, but not from the pain of bruised ribs.

"Hey, I was—" Georgia said, stepping around the curtain. "Sorry, I didn't mean to interrupt."

Lana ignored her. "Garrett, you'll at least talk to Sketch before you leave?"

Garrett studied the contents of the envelope. "Yep."

She didn't move for a second, then quietly walked away. He closed his eyes, taking a deep breath to calm his pulse. There was no other way for this to end.

"Uh…what was that about?" Georgia said.

"Nothing you need to concern yourself with, Agent Hunt."

"Bet you'll be glad to get out of here and enjoy your leave of absence."

"You have no idea." He handed her the file, a prop to keep Lana at a distance.

"Sorry I didn't listen to you about your Port Whisper suspicions."

"You had evidence leading you in a different direction. You had to follow it."

"I should have respected your instinct. You're a master at this job. Speaking of which, when are you returning to the team?"

"Not sure. I think I deserve a vacation, don't you?"

"Yeah, right. You'll be bored in forty-eight hours. You can't live without it."

Maybe she was right. But for once in his life he wanted to try.

If only it could be with Lana.

SIXTEEN

The next morning, Garrett headed out early to the police station to wrap things up with Morgan.

"So he left the bottle, cigar and belt on the victims because…?" Morgan asked.

"The booze and cigar were his stepfather's favorite brands and the belt was the weapon he used on Anderson. His stepfather was already dead, but once Dianna's death triggered his killing instinct, Jack relived the fantasy of killing him over and over."

"He was one sick guy."

"That, he was."

"You're lucky he didn't kill you at the lighthouse."

"Thanks to Lana." She'd elbowed Anderson, giving Garrett the chance to take him down. Only, Garrett never expected the guy to actually jump from the gallery to his death.

"I'm glad it's over," Morgan said. "You do good work, Agent Drake."

"Thanks, Morgan. One thing we never discussed was the Pete Lonergan situation," Garrett said. "There has to be something we can do to stop him from bullying kids in town."

"It's handled. My wife and your—" He hesitated. "Julie and Lana have convinced Pete's parents to send him on a church mission trip to India next month."

"Now there's punishment. Two weeks without Xbox or internet."

"Actually, Lana doesn't see it as punishment. She thinks the experience will open his heart. Her words. I call it a reality check."

"Leave it to Lana." He smiled and shook his head.

The door to the police station swung open, and Sketch stormed over to Garrett. "What are you doing?"

"Wrapping things up with Morgan. Why, what are you doing?"

"Trying to keep my girlfriend from completely freaking out, thanks to you."

Garrett and Morgan exchanged glances.

"And how did I upset your girlfriend?" Garrett asked.

"Ashley said you haven't talked to Lana since you guys were almost killed at the lighthouse."

"That is accurate."

"Why not?" his son challenged.

"That's between Lana and me."

"You mean it's between you and you? Because Lana has no idea why you're ignoring her."

"We were connected because of the case. The case is over, therefore our relationship is over. Trust me, it's for the best."

"Really?" He glared at Garrett, waiting.

"What do you want me to say, Steven?"

"Forget it." He marched to the door, hesitated and spun around, pinning Garrett with angry eyes. "Ya know, I'm sorry I got to know you as my dad because I had this fantasy that my real dad was some kind of superhero. But you're not a superhero. You're a coward, just like Morgan."

"Hey," Morgan protested.

"Sorry, I mean, you were a coward, but you're not a coward anymore, Chief."

"Thank you." Morgan leaned back in his chair.

Sketch shook his head at Garrett. "You're avoiding Lana because the emotion thing is hard, probably harder than your job where you fly all over the country and look at dead bodies," he said, motioning with his hand. "So keep doing that, Dad. Keep running away from your life and probably the best thing that's happened to you since I was born."

Sketch marched out of the police station and silence rang in Garrett's ears. He glanced sideways at Morgan.

"Yeah, he's really good at the guilt thing," Morgan said.

"I need to get out of this town." Garrett ran his hand across his face.

"You can do that, but you won't stop thinking about her."

"Is it that obvious?"

"Nah, not at all." Morgan grinned.

With a sigh, Garrett glanced blindly across the room. "Lana and me… It's a bad idea."

"You sure? Or did your kid nail it and you're scared?"

"What have I got to be scared of?"

"Oh, I don't know, maybe breaking down those walls that protect you from your job?"

"You know this is impossible, what with my job and her living here and—"

"Hey, you don't have to have all the answers right now. Just the answer to one, very important question. Do you care about her?"

"Yeah, I do."

"Okay, so what are you gonna do about it?"

It was the first tour since Salish Island had reopened. As Lana steered her boat across the calm waters, she absently rattled off stories about Port Whisper and the island.

She left out the part about falling in love with an honorable, stubborn man, about cradling his head in her lap and praying he'd open his eyes and say her name.

She wished she could forget him, but some things stuck with you and were embedded in your heart. Odd that she didn't feel nearly this much pain when she and Vincent had split up.

Maybe because that wasn't real love.

"Lana?" Ashley prompted.

Lana glanced at her, then over her shoulder at the group of sixteen tourists, and realized she'd stopped talking midsentence. "Sorry," she apologized. "I'm distracted by this beautiful day. I'd better focus on docking."

She redirected her attention to the island ahead and spotted the police boat tied up at the dock. "I wonder what's going on?"

"I heard they were wrapping things up," Ashley offered.

"You heard?" Lana eyed her. "Tell that boyfriend of yours to stop eavesdropping on private conversations between the chief and his staff."

"He can't help it if they talk work stuff when he's helping Morgan with computer stuff."

"Sketch misses his dad, doesn't he?" Lana assumed Garrett had left town as soon as possible. After all, he had a case in Ohio to investigate.

Ashley shrugged. "I'll tie us off."

"Thanks." Her gaze followed her teenage assistant who'd been awfully quiet today. Sketch's mood must have rubbed off on her.

It probably didn't help that Lana was in a funk, but she was allowed, considering Garrett had completely shut her out. He'd decided there was no possibility of a future between them, and that was that. No discussion, no appeal on her part, because she wouldn't beg him to like her.

She didn't have to. She knew he liked her.

It was something else that made him run, and not just another case. Who knows, maybe it was the irrational fear that he'd hurt her. Wait, not so irrational considering he already had.

She cut the engine and Ashley wrapped the ropes around the metal cleats. As the tourists filed off the boat, they each grabbed a white sack lunch from a bin. She glanced across the island, a wealth of serenity and natural beauty. Even after everything that had happened—the dead body floating up on shore and Lana almost being killed—she clung to the pleasant memories of this enchanting island. She would not let the ugliness taint her perspective of this beautiful place.

"Feel free to walk around the island and find a nice spot to eat lunch," Lana said. "Our two rules are to stay on this side of the bank of trees so we don't disturb the wildlife, and please do not litter. Enjoy."

The group dispersed and Lana headed in the opposite direction. She'd been forcing a smile all morning, and needed a break.

"Where are you going?" Ashley asked.

"Down by the water."

"Oh." Ashley rocked back and forth on her heels. "You're acting weird."

"Waiting for Sketch to—" She ripped her phone out of her pocket. "It's him."

As she dashed off, Lana spotted Morgan and Julie walking toward her, holding hands. An ache spiked through her chest at the memory of how Garrett's hand had felt in hers. She cleared her throat. "Hey, what are you guys doing out here?"

"Needed some alone time," Julie said. "I'd ask how you're doing, but I have a feeling you're sick of that question."

"Right on, big sister." She glanced at Morgan. "Have you seen Garrett?"

"I have."

"Is he, you know, okay?"

Morgan and Julie shared an awkward glance.

"Ah, never mind. Weird question. None of my business anyway. I'm gonna…" she pointed behind her "…take a walk."

"You want company?" Julie asked.

"Jules," Morgan said with warning in his voice. He knew how Lana hated the smothering business.

"No, I need to think," Lana said. "See you guys later."

She offered the best smile in her arsenal, but since Garrett had shut her out, none of her smiles seemed all that genuine.

Lana wandered down the trail to the rocky beach. The sound of water creeping up the shore and back into the Sound always brought her peace.

As she made the final turn to the shoreline, she spotted a man sitting on a rock. She almost thought it was Garrett, except that he was wearing jeans and a cargo jacket. Garrett never wore anything but sharply pressed suits, even when he was officially on his leave of absence.

She really wanted to be alone, so she turned around and started back up the trail.

"Lana?"

She froze. She turned around and her breath caught at the sight of Garrett, standing there, looking at her.

"What are you doing here?" she said.

"Waiting for you."

"How did you know I'd come down here?"

"I didn't. I was…" He shoved his hands into his jeans pockets. "Trying to build up the courage to go find you."

"You needed courage to talk to me?"

"Yep."

"Why?"

"After the way I acted at the hospital…" His voice trailed off. "I've been told I'm a coward."

"Let me guess, Sketch?"

"Yes, ma'am."

"He's a smart kid, like his dad."

"Not so smart when it comes to the important stuff."

She held her breath, her heart pounding in her chest. "Keep talking."

"Aw, this is so awkward."

She ambled toward him. "It doesn't have to be. Just say what's in your heart."

"I thought I was protecting you by pushing you away after the case was over, but I was doing it again…. Running. So, I've decided to stop and enjoy what my son referred to as *the best thing that's happened to me since he was born.*"

"How humble of him."

Garrett actually smiled. She couldn't remember seeing him fully smile like this. It was a beautiful sight.

"I'm really not good at this," he said, glancing down.

She took another few steps and wrapped her arms around his waist. "Actually, I think you're great at his. I mean, if you're trying to tell me you want to date me."

"Date you?" He looked straight into her eyes. "Wow, o people still do that?"

"They certainly do. It would be nice to spend some me together when we're not in mortal danger."

"I was kinda hoping you'd say that." He took her and and led her down the beach.

She didn't know where they were going and she idn't care. Garrett was here, holding her hand, try-ng his best to tell her that he cared about her, maybe ven loved her.

They turned a corner, and she spotted a blanket pread across a large, smooth rock. A picnic basket entered the blanket.

"Hey, I'm on duty, Agent Drake," she said. "I've got boat full of people to tend to."

"Which is why your sister and Morgan are here."

"They helped you plan this?"

"They did."

"Julie must have changed her mind about you."

"I think Morgan had something to do with that. A ecture about giving people second chances, some-hing like that."

"Way to go, Morgan," Lana whispered and glanced ut across the calm waters. "If the tide shifts, we could e in trouble."

"A little water doesn't scare me." He turned to her. "But you do."

She started to ask why and he pressed his forefin-

ger to her lips. "I haven't been in a serious relation
ship since my marriage. This thing between us coul
be an illusion, something created by the adrenalin
wave we've been riding this past week. I keep tellin
myself that because the alternative is, well, it's rea
and I'm completely baffled by what to do with that.'

"You mean the fact we've fallen in love?"

"Yeah."

"I'll tell you what to do. Kiss me."

Garrett leaned forward and pressed a sweet, gen
tle kiss on her lips. He broke the kiss and breathe
against her cheek.

"Still scared?" she said.

"Terrified."

"Don't worry. I'll protect you."

* * * * *

Dear Reader,

I'm pleased to share with you the third book in my Port Whisper series. It was such fun to revisit the charming town with familiar friends like the Burns family, along with one of my all-time-favorite characters, the bright and precocious teenager Steven Drake aka Sketch.

What was most interesting to me was writing about Sketch's father, FBI profiler Garrett Drake, who made a choice thirteen years ago to separate from his wife and young son in order to protect them. It's a decision he's regretted every day of his life. Yet in my mind, clinging to regret only bruises your soul, it doesn't nourish it. We all make mistakes, and we pray for forgiveness. Hopefully we learn from those mistakes and make better decisions the next time around. And even if we don't, well, that's the beauty of being human.

Through family and community, Garrett learns to surrender his regret, and open his heart to hope, love and God, all while protecting his son and the woman he loves from a killer. He's on a remarkable journey, one I hope you enjoy as much as I did.

Peace,
Hope White

Questions for Discussion

1. Do you think Garrett was right to send his family away when he became a target of a serial killer?

2. Do you think Garrett should have fought harder to stay a part of his son's life? Why or why not?

3. How do you think Garrett's abandonment of his son affected Sketch?

4. What strengths do you think Lana brought to her relationship with Garrett?

5. Do you think Lana stayed in Port Whisper out of fear or love, and why?

6. Have you ever made a decision based on fear? And if so, what did you learn, if anything, from making that kind of decision?

7. Have you ever known anyone like Caroline, who held on to her resentment like a warm blanket in wintertime? How do you think holding on to resentment affects a person?

8. If you've ever been resentful, and unable to let it go, what did you do to ease the pain in your heart? Did you consult favorite Bible verses, and if so which ones?

9. If Sketch wouldn't have forgiven and accepted his father, do you think Garrett should have kept trying? Why or why not?

0. Did you admire Lana's strength, fueled by her faith? What things help you focus on being in a state of grace?

1. Do you think Lana's mom and sister were justified in being overly protective of Lana? Why or why not?

2. Did Garrett push Lana away in the end because he thought it was the best for Lana, or because he was scared of getting emotionally involved?

13. Do you think some people, like the killer in this book, are born "bad" or do other things contribute to their darkness?

14. If Garrett hadn't been reunited with his son, how do you think the rest of his life would have turned out?

LARGER-PRINT BOOKS!

GET 2 FREE
LARGER-PRINT NOVELS
PLUS 2 FREE
MYSTERY GIFTS

Love Inspired®

SUSPENSE
RIVETING INSPIRATIONAL ROMANCE

Larger-print novels are now available...

YES! Please send me 2 FREE LARGER-PRINT Love Inspired® Suspense novels and my 2 FREE mystery gifts (gifts are worth about $10). After receiving them, if I don't wish to receive any more books, I can return the shipping statement marked "cancel". If I don't cancel, I will receive 4 brand-new novels every month and be billed just $4.99 per book in the U.S. or $5.49 per book in Canada. That's a saving of at least 23% off the cover price. It's quite a bargain! Shipping and handling is just 50¢ per book in the U.S. and 75¢ per book in Canada.* I understand that accepting the 2 free books and gifts places me under no obligation to buy anything. I can always return a shipment and cancel at any time. Even if I never buy another book, the two free books and gifts are mine to keep forever.

110/310 IDN FEH3

Name _____ (PLEASE PRINT) _____

Address _____ Apt. # _____

City _____ State/Prov. _____ Zip/Postal Code _____

Signature (if under 18, a parent or guardian must sign)

Mail to the **Reader Service:**
IN U.S.A.: P.O. Box 1867, Buffalo, NY 14240-1867
IN CANADA: P.O. Box 609, Fort Erie, Ontario L2A 5X3

Not valid for current subscribers to Love Inspired Suspense larger-print books.

**Are you a current subscriber to Love Inspired Suspense books
and want to receive the larger-print edition?
Call 1-800-873-8635 or visit www.ReaderService.com.**

* Terms and prices subject to change without notice. Prices do not include applicable taxes. Sales tax applicable in N.Y. Canadian residents will be charged applicable taxes. Offer not valid in Quebec. This offer is limited to one order per household. All orders subject to credit approval. Credit or debit balances in a customer's account(s) may be offset by any other outstanding balance owed by or to the customer. Please allow 4 to 6 weeks for delivery. Offer available while quantities last.

Your Privacy—The Reader Service is committed to protecting your privacy. Our Privacy Policy is available online at www.ReaderService.com or upon request from the Reader Service.

We make a portion of our mailing list available to reputable third parties that offer products we believe may interest you. If you prefer that we not exchange your name with third parties, or if you wish to clarify or modify your communication preferences, please visit us at www.ReaderService.com/consumerchoice or write to us at Reader Service Preference Service, P.O. Box 9062, Buffalo, NY 14269. Include your complete name and address.

LISUSLP11B

LARGER-PRINT BOOKS!

**GET 2 FREE
LARGER-PRINT NOVELS
PLUS 2 FREE
MYSTERY GIFTS**

Larger-print novels are now available...